Twits to the Test

A STEAMPUNK DISTRACTION

TOM ALAN ROBBINS

BOOK SIX OF THE TWITS CHRONICLES

Claim A Free Gift!

Visit Twitschronicles.com to claim a free copy of the Twits short story *Uncle Hugo's Crisis.* Or, if you are reading this on a device, you can click HERE.

What People Are Saying:

"The Twits Chronicles are hilarious, blessed with truly exceptional dialogue. Steampunk dystopia meets Oscar Wildean wit in these books. I found myself laughing out loud on numerous occasions--and that's not something I often do while reading. "

—Nick Sullivan, author of The Deep Series and Zombie Bigfoot.

"Delightful! A frothy frappe of P.G. Wodehouse and steam-punk. If you're the sort who reads blurbs before reading the book, stop it. Stop it right now. Read TWITS IN LOVE and have a good time. These days we can all use a bit more of a good time."

—John Ostrander, American writer of comic books, including *Suicide Squad, Grimjack* and *Star Wars: Legacy*.

"I haven't enjoyed the company of such eccentric characters since A Confederacy of Dunces, and Tom Alan Robbins has managed to place them in the stylized world of Oscar Wilde. A really unique journey."

— Kevin Conroy, Actor, The voice behind the DC Comics superhero Batman .

"Tom Alan Robbins' Twits stories are hilarious, thought provoking and mind bending. His juicy turns of phrase will stick in your ear like a catchy song."

— Michael Urie, Actor, Producer and Director

"Tom is the most talented, delicious writer. Do yourself a favor, and immerse yourself in the fabulous world of TWITS!"

— Mary Testa, 3 time Tony Award Nominee

The Author makes no representation of any kind as to his being a citizen of the United Kingdom, either native or naturalized. He is from a small town in Ohio, for which he apologizes.

Copyright © 2022 by Tom Alan Robbins

This is a work of fiction. All events described are imaginary; all characters are entirely fictitious and are not intended to represent actual living persons.

Cover design by Melody J. Barber of Aurora Publicity

Additional designs by Eric Wright of The Puppet Kitchen.

Twits Logo designed by Feppa Rodriquez

Proofreading by Gretchen Tannert Douglas

For Margot Harley, friend and mentor, without whom my life would certainly have taken a different (and far less joyous) path.

Steampunk

"Steampunk is a subgenre of science fiction that incorporates retrofuturistic technology and aesthetics inspired by 19th-century industrial steam-powered machinery. Steampunk works are often set in an alternative history of the Victorian era or the American "Wild West", where steam power remains in mainstream use, or in a fantasy world that similarly employs steam power."

Wikipedia

A Word About Timelines

For those who are unfamiliar with the Steampunk genre, a word about timelines may be helpful. The Steampunk Universe in which The Twits Chronicles take place is clearly not our own. That is why events and cultural references that clearly happened in vastly different eras in our own world seem to happen in a compressed time period. It feels as if we are in a vaguely Victorian era, and yet there are references to events and quotations from well into the twentieth century.

It may help to think of this as an exercise in "what if?" What if electricity wasn't discovered until much later in human history? Human ingenuity would still search for new ways of using existing technology, and so steam power and mechanical engineering would keep advancing, while much of the aesthetic of the world around us could remain in the nineteenth century.

The world that would result is the world of The Twits Chronicles. Other writers would use these same criteria to create very different realities. This is mine.

Enter and enjoy.

Contents

CHAPTER ONE

The Curse of Caspar Haspenhausen

I did not wish to live.

"Bentley," I managed to croak, "Help!"

Charles Barnswoggle is a git. I say it, and I stand by it. It was he who had introduced the gang to something called a "mai tai" at the club the previous evening. Now the rosy beams of the inevitable morning found me locked in a paroxysm of pain that made all previous hangovers seem like hangnails. I hazily recalled a limbo contest, breaking glass and gigantic teeth giving one the hee-haw.

"Bentley?" I lay still and waited for the dependable entrance of my mechanical valet.

There would be aspirin and hair of the dog. Bentley would save me. Minutes passed and the only thing that danced attendance were the dust motes in the sunbeams. Comprehension suddenly burst through the alcoholic fog. An icy hand grasped my vitals. I had forgotten that this was the one day of the year when Bentley returned to the factory for an inspection. I was alone!

You will observe, quite rightly, that I should have been prepared. The date had been circled by Bentley on a large calendar which he had hung by my bedside the previous evening.

"You will recall, Sir, that I shall not be here to attend on you tomorrow?"

"Yes, yes, Bentley. I shall be quite all right."

"May I suggest once again that you forgo any carousing at the club tonight? I will not be in a position to post bail or to suture any wounds you may receive."

"Good heavens, I'm not a child. I'm quite capable of taking care of myself."

I had spoken with all the confidence of youth, but my cousin Binky had convinced me that there was nothing sinister about a little game of bridge in the card room. Barnswoggle had turned up with those misbegotten mai tais and here I was.

Think... I must think! I squinted at the clock on the wall—seven fifty-nine. The morning cannons would thunder forth in one minute! I knew from past hangovers how devastating their reverberations could be.

"Steady, Old Boy," I murmured to myself. Moving at a glacial pace, I extended a shaking arm and managed to hook a nearby pillow. I labouriously dragged it toward me and pulled it over my head just as the cannons up and down the road went off with a roar! Despite the muting effects of the poly-fill, the pain was indescribable! I breathed deeply and managed to slow the old ticker. First crisis averted. Now, what to do about my swelling bladder?

I was just reaching out a claw to grasp the blanket when I heard the front doorbell. I had been convinced by a fast-talking salesperson that musical doorbells were going to be all the rage this season but was growing devilishly tired of hearing "Lady of Spain" every time someone yanked the cord. Whoever was at the door wouldn't take no for a bloody answer. "Lady of Spain" must have played through five or six times before a blessed silence fell—then, to my horror, I heard the front door creak! I heard footsteps on the stairs! The bedroom door slowly opened and who should enter the boudoir but my Aunt Hypatia! Well, this was too much. I closed my eyes and gave myself up for lost.

"There you are, Nephew. What are you doing in bed? The morning cannons have sounded. Live free or die."

My aunt's voice has been compared to a trumpet. I would have said a steam whistle on a tugboat, but I am not impartial.

"Can't speak, Aunt... sick."

"Sick? Nonsense. Wellness is an act of will! You must will yourself out of bed and you will see how much better you feel."

"Can't move... hurts."

"Where does it hurt?"

"Everywhere."

She came nearer and peered at me intently. She sniffed suspiciously. "Have you been drinking?"

"Not at all. Perhaps I had a beer."

"The alcohol is positively leaking out of your pores. You have a hangover."

"It is possible."

"Your Uncle Hugo used to suffer from that condition. I cured him of it. He has not touched a drop in twenty years."

"Poor Uncle," I murmured sympathetically, while recalling that same uncle with a mai tai in each fist at the club the previous evening.

"Don't feel sorry for him. He feels sorry enough for himself."

There was something nagging at me from a far corner of what remained of my mind. I looked up at my aunt suspiciously. "I say, Aunt, how did you get in? Bentley would never have left the front door unlocked."

"Of course not. I have a key."

I sputtered a bit. "What ho? How did you acquire such a thing?"

"I have had it for years. Your parents gave it to me before they departed. They asked me to keep an eye on you."

The mention of my parents caused me to sink deeper into my pillows. "That was thoughtful. They must have had a premonition of their impending demise."

My Aunt started and stared at me strangely. "Demise, you say?"

"Yes—how I wish they were still here to see the man I have become."

She avoided my gaze and stared at the china figurines on the nightstand. "Did Bentley tell you of their... egress?"

"He did, when I was old enough to comprehend it."

"What did he say, exactly?"

"That they were departed."

"Yes, that is undeniably accurate. You're certain that he did not say that they 'had' departed?"

"'Were', 'had', they are much the same thing. You're acting rather oddly, Aunt. Is there something you wish to tell me?"

She regained her equilibrium. "No, no... well, since I'm here, is there anything I can do to assist you?"

"You couldn't help me up, could you? I need to use the... um... facility."

"Why don't I find a bowl that you could use as a bedpan?"

"I think not."

"I have experience. During the war I held many a bedpan. I have always thought it was excellent training for serving punch at cricket matches—the cut crystal bowl with all that liquid sloshing about."

"Perhaps another time. If you could just remove the bedclothes from atop me and give me a boost, I think I could make it on my own."

"Very well."

She peeled back the linens with a surprisingly gentle touch and took my hand. I have always suspected that Aunt Hypatia lifts weights when no one is watching and, indeed, she pulled me to my feet like I was a kitten.

"Thanks awfully." I tottered to the bathroom, did the necessary and returned to find her holding a brimming cup that looked surprisingly familiar. "I say, is that..."

"Bentley's morning after concoction. I found it under the shirt that you had flung so cavalierly onto the dresser. There was a note. It said, "In case of emergencies."

"'Give me. Tell me not of fear.'" I seized the glass and downed it in one gulp. My headache began to fade away and the room ceased to spin.

"Do you know," my aunt mused, "I rather miss taking care of someone. Hugo is so self-sufficient. Would you like me to make you something to eat?"

"You can cook?" I couldn't have been more amazed if she had risen into the air and flown about the room.

"Of course I can cook. I didn't always have servants."

"Didn't you?"

"The family thought that young people should learn to be self-reliant. We weren't allowed servants until we reached the age of twelve. I can heat packaged dinners and even construct the occasional sandwich."

"You're full of surprises."

She eyed me with amusement. "Not quite the dragon you imagined me to be?"

"Not at all. I say, this is rather jolly. What brought you to *mi casa* on this particular morning?"

Her eyes suddenly skittered away from mine and she became fascinated by the plaster moldings around the doorway. "Oh... nothing really. I did want to ask a teensy favour..."

I felt a tingle at the back of my neck that invariably signaled approaching danger. "Oh? Pray tell, what is this service that you require?"

"Well... I would very much appreciate it if you would sponsor your cousin Caspar Haspenhausen for membership at the club."

"Who, Caspar the Delinquent Ghost?" I stared at her in shock. "The members would never forgive me! Don't ask it of me, Aunt, please!"

She rose from her chair and towered over me. "What is wrong with Caspar? His lineage is every bit as elevated as your own."

"But he's a cyst, Aunt. You know he is! He's famous for disappearing whenever a bill is due and his idea of fun would embarrass a drunken Visigoth. I've lost count of the times Bentley has had to bail him out of the pokey for knocking down some poor unsuspecting police person or for heckling a parson during his Easter sermon."

"Youthful spirits!"

"Spirits are certainly at fault."

"He is your cousin. That trumps all of his supposed flaws."

"Why can't Uncle Hugo sponsor him? He's a member."

"There are procedural reasons, which your uncle has explained to me."

I suddenly saw a glimmer of hope. "But Aunt, Caspar can't be a member, you know. He's not a firstborn son."

For those of you unfamiliar with the bylaws of my club, Twits, a new member must be the firstborn son of an existing member. This may seem overly restrictive but the benefits of club membership are so overwhelming that if it were open to all and sundry there would be a tidal wave of applicants that would swamp our little paradise.

I lay back and wallowed in self-satisfaction. Bentley could not have handled it more neatly. My aunt, however, showed no signs of retreat.

"You are aware that Twits was founded by your great-great-grandfather, Percy Chippington-Smythe?"

"Yes, bless him—founder of the family fortune."

"Your uncle has explained to me that in the club charter Percy reserved certain unique powers for himself."

"Did he? He must have been a Byzantine sort of fellow."

"What you are perhaps unaware of is that these unique powers pass down through his male line."

"Do they? Most interesting," I yawned.

"The current representative of that male line is... you."

"Yes, I quite see that. Thank you for explaining."

"And among the unique powers that you possess is the power to open the membership of Twits to individuals who do not meet the criteria set forth in the charter."

This seemed to be taking an unfortunate turn. "Sorry, wha-what?" I stammered.

"Simply put, you are the only person with the power to nominate your cousin Caspar for membership."

I shot upright. "Well really! This hardly seems fair. What was Great-great-grandfather thinking? If I nominate The Ghost I'll be a pariah!"

"Nevertheless."

"Wait a moment, though... they'll still have to vote on it, won't they? He'll never get past the committee."

"We shall cross that bridge when we come to it. Your job is to propose him. Can I depend on you?"

My mind raced madly to and fro, throwing itself at the bars of its cell, trying to find a way out. Alas, there was no escape. I smiled weakly at my aunt. "Always happy to help."

She harrumphed with satisfaction and prepared to weigh anchor. "When does Bentley return?"

"This evening."

"Try to stay alive until then."

"I shall do my best."

She gathered up her skirts and swept out of the room. I lay back in the bed, feeling that on the whole, things could have been worse. The membership committee would certainly vote Caspar down post haste. Thanks to Bentley's elixir, the headache was gone. My bladder was empty and the world was my oyster, if oysters still roamed the deep. Time to greet the new day.

Showering was not an insurmountable obstacle. I had observed Bentley adjusting the temperature by fiddling with those round thingies labeled H and C (the initials of the manufacturer, one supposed). After fifteen minutes or so of trial and error the water became just warm enough for a quick duck and a dab at the nether regions. Shaving presented a more serious challenge. I found a note in Bentley's hand where the razor usually resided.

"Sir," it read, "I have taken the liberty of concealing your razor for obvious reasons. Please make arrangements to be shaved at the club."

So that was all right. My clothes for the day were thoughtfully laid out, and after substituting a charming pink cravat with a pattern of yellow daffodils for the dull thing that Bentley had intended, I contemplated the structural undergarments that would buttress my superstructure and give form to chaos. Compression stockings were child's play... but the corset... I had never really examined it before. Bentley strapped me into it each morning but for the life of me I couldn't remember the actual process. I normally stood and daydreamed the morning away while Bentley bustled around me cinching this and buckling that. There were laces up the back, but how was one to tie them? My arms would never reach so far. I let the thing dangle and concentrated furiously. If I left the laces tied, I might be able to wriggle into it like a snake. I saw no other alternative. I slipped my arms into the bottom of the corset and raised them over my head. It slid down to my shoulders, which left my arms trapped above me. I began to undulate madly and managed to get the thing halfway down my chest but there it stuck and no amount of shimmying would budge it. I decided to retreat but found that the blasted thing wouldn't go up or down. I stumbled about the room a bit and finally tripped onto the bed. I lay still and indulged in a round of self-pity. I supposed that Bentley would find me here when he returned in the evening. He would exhibit no satisfaction at my total dependence on him, but I knew that it would be entered into his data banks to be pulled out at a later date as the *coup de grace* in a disagreement over shoes or ketchup or some such item of contention. I sighed and would have wiped a moist eye if my arms were not hopelessly pinioned above me.

After a few minutes of this, my stomach began to growl. I had not considered that in my present condition I would go hungry until Bentley's return. Cook was away visiting a sick relative so there was no help to be had from that quarter. I had heard that hunger was an agonizing condition although I had never experienced it myself. I was certainly not going to suffer such a fate without a fight! Exerting a superhuman effort I rolled myself to the side of the bed and dropped onto the carpet with a thump. Using my knees and elbows I began to inch like a caterpillar toward what I hoped was the door. I had a vague, half-formed plan to reach the kitchen and to attempt to funnel something edible down the canvas tube and into my waiting mouth. I was able to see a tiny circle of my surroundings through my twisted arms. I headed for the hallway, only to find my way blocked by a pair of patent leather boots. This was odd, since I don't possess a pair of patent leather boots.

A voice issued from somewhere above said boots. It sounded very much like my feckless cousin, Binky.

"What on earth are you up to?"

"Binky, is that you?"

"Is it some sort of game? Can I play?"

"It's not a game. I've got this bloody corset stuck on my head. See if you can pull it off."

"Why don't you just unzip it?"

"What? Is there a zipper?"

"Certainly. It runs up the side."

"I didn't see it."

"Have you never put on a corset before?"

"Not by myself, no."

"Very well. Give me half a mo'."

There was some fumbling at my tubular prison, a loud zipping sound and the blessed light of day shone on my grateful face. "Thanks awfully."

"Not at all. You'd do as much for me."

"At any time."

"Need a hand up?"

"Please."

"Clap on, then."

He hauled me to my feet and we stood awkwardly for a moment trying to regain our equilibrium.

"Live free or die."

"Live free or die."

A thought struck me. "Say, how did you get into the house?"

"Your front door was wide open. I thought perhaps there were burglars."

"That was Aunt Hypatia. She is not accustomed to closing doors. Or opening them for that matter."

"What on earth did she want?"

I stared at him gloomily. "You might as well be the first to know. She's got me proposing my cousin Caspar for membership at Twits."

"The Delinquent Ghost? That will make you persona non grata."

"Don't I know it, but what can I do? You know my aunt."

"But look here... he's not a firstborn son, is he?"

"That's the devil of it. Apparently, I inherited the power through my great-great-grandfather to propose anyone for membership, including any lunatic, criminal or actor you care to name."

"Diabolical," he breathed. "It's a sort of family curse. You must never procreate. The horror must end with you."

"Agreed, but that doesn't solve my immediate problem."

"Look here, I'll go with you for moral support. It's best to do it quickly, like ripping off a bandage. The Ghost will never make it past the committee. It will all be over by lunchtime."

He was right, of course. I dressed quickly—the corset was a piece of cake once one knew its secret—and we trotted down to the garage. I was driving an unobtrusive black town car these days to avoid the censure of the protesting class, but inside its dull exterior I was still able to exercise my creative bent. This week the theme was the reign of Pope Julius II, and the Sistine Chapel frescoes covered the roof and side pillars in a riot of colour. One touched the finger of God in the center of the roof to start the car. I extended my forefinger and completed the circuit. We were off!

CHAPTER TWO

The Best Laid Plans

Upon arriving at Twits, I tossed the keys to Evans, the doorman. "Good morning, Evans. Is the committee meeting this morning?"

He gazed inward at his memory banks and I heard something click within him. "Yes, Sir. They are in the conference room until eleven o'clock."

"Good-oh. Come on, Binky."

As we headed into the lobby, I spied Cheeseworth—one of the club's charming eccentrics. He was attended by two oddly encumbered individuals. One carried a pad of paper on which he was madly sketching, and the other wore a long vest covered with what looked like small trash bags. This individual was pulling scraps of paper out of his pocket and scribbling on them, then depositing them into one trash bag or other according to some system known only to himself.

"Hallo, Cheeseworth!" I waved at him cheerfully.

The gentleman with the sketch pad ripped off the top page, studied me intently for a moment and began sketching. The other fellow pulled out a scrap of paper and began scribbling, speaking loudly as he did so.

"Cyril Chippington-Smythe needs a shave! Trashbag, 'stubble in paradise?'" He then selected a bag hanging by his left hip and shoved the scrap of paper into it.

I stared at Cheeseworth. "What on earth is all this?"

He simpered at me. "This is my social media team. They wecord the events of my day and disseminate it to the public at large."

The sketch artist had ripped off the page and dropped it at my feet before beginning another frantic caricature. I picked it up and studied it. He had captured my ears, but the nose seemed unnecessarily pointy. "Does the public at large enjoy this sort of thing?"

The fellow with the bags hollered, "Chippington-Smythe questions public's taste.

Trashbag, 'let them eat cake'?" He shoved this scrap into yet another sack.

"They simply eat it up," gloated Cheeseworth. "They have an insatiable appetite for anything that offers a glimpse into the minutiae of a celebrity's life."

"Are you a celebrity, then?"

"I shall be soon, thanks to the welentless flogging of my media team."

The fellow with the vest scribbled while yelling, "Cheeseworth thanks media team! Gives them full credit. Trashbag, 'media is the message'!" He popped the scribble into a bag.

Binky had been watching all this with eyes wide. "Where did you get them? They're terribly agitating."

Cheeseworth leaned in confidentially. "Do you remember the Social Media King?"

Of course, it was impossible to forget that shady entrepreneur of malicious gossip. We had met him on an adventure in New York City and had narrowly escaped being ensnared in his web.

Cheeseworth gestured to his team to put down their pencils for a moment. "Well, we've corresponded a few times regarding some shared interests in how to pwotect one's identity from being discov... er... stolen. He sent these fellows to me as a gesture of thanks for some of my suggestions. Aren't they too divine?"

"I suppose, if you like that sort of thing," I replied dubiously.

Binky was looking around. "I say, where are your sheep, Cheeseworth?"

Cheeseworth had been renting a small flock of sheep, played by actors of course, as pets. I had grown rather fond of Compton, the ram of the flock.

"Gone!" Cheeseworth cried pettishly. "They were offered a tour of Thoroughly Modern Millie and left me in the lurch. I shall never trust a sheep again—tweacherous cweatures!"

The sketch artist revved up, and the scribbler began to scribble again. "Sheep are traitors, says Cheeseworth! Trashbag, 'unreliable ruminants'."

My head was beginning to throb. "Sorry, Cheeseworth... it's a little much at this hour of the morning. I've got to run."

"Of course. Ta-ta, lads."

Binky and I wove our way through the lobby toward the conference room but were stopped short by the appearance of Mrs. Beasely, the club cat, who stalked into the corridor and stood glaring at us like a clergyman glaring at an empty collection box. She arched her back and hissed. We retreated a step.

"Is there another way to reach the conference room?"

Binky shook his head. "You used to be able to cut through the tea room but that door was walled up when they put in the new gift shop."

Mrs. Beasely extended her claws and inched forward. We took another step back.

If you have never met Mrs. Beasely, you can consider yourself fortunate indeed. Because of their proximity to people, cats and dogs are among the few animals that survived The Great Extinction. This has given them an exalted position among the populace, who have an insatiable appetite for being near things that they can feel superior to. As the club cat, Mrs. Beasely was doubly esteemed. She had the full run of Twits and woe betide the member who tried to evict her from a comfy chair by the fire. You could find one or two unlucky sorts in the dining room any day of the week sporting wicked scratches on their cheeks.

I looked around for Evans, the doorman, who could usually be found wandering the lobby.

He paced over and took in the situation. "She seems to have made herself at home, Sir."

"But I have to get to the conference room, Evans. Can't you move her?"

"Alas, I have strict instructions not to interfere with Mrs. Beasely, but I keep a can of cat food and a can opener at my station. They are at your disposal."

He retrieved the items specified and paced away. Mrs. Beasely watched me through slitted eyes. I stared at the can opener, then at the can, but could discern no relationship between them that would lead to the unveiling of the cat food inside.

Binky watched me struggle and gave a sigh. "Let me do it. You really are too helpless."

He performed some sort of legerdemain with the can opener and the scent of cat food bloomed in the lobby. He placed the can to one side of the corridor. Mrs. Beasely looked at the can, then at us, then at the can. Finally, she gave a catlike shrug and padded over to bury her face in our offering and we scampered by her.

We pulled up in front of the conference room. Binky brushed some lint from my shoulder.

"Just say it quickly. They'll holler for a while, then vote him down and we can have a bite of breakfast."

I squared my shoulders and knocked. The door was opened by an ancient member wearing the ceremonial fez of the committee.

"We are in session, Mr. Chippington-Smythe. Come back later."

"I have business with the committee, Mr. Nosegurgle. Please announce me."

He glared at me with bloodshot eyes and turned away. "Mr. Chippington-Smythe wishes to be heard."

There was some indistinct grumbling from within and the door was opened just wide enough to admit me. The committee sat at a long table covered with brandy bottles and cigars. The members in their fezzes were uniformly ancient and ill-tempered. The head of the committee was Griffin Scabies. His eyes were almost totally obscured by his enormous eyebrows and his lips by a pendulous mustache. It was like being spoken to by the pile of sweepings in a barber shop.

"This had better be important, Chippington-Smythe. We were just about to have our brandy."

"Well... I wouldn't say important. I'm sure we can dispose of this in a moment. It's just... I wonder if I might propose Caspar Haspenhausen for membership? It's fine if you'd rather not. I just thought I'd mention it."

There was a moment of stunned silence before the room exploded in a yowl that sounded like a herd of cats being roasted. The Head pounded his fist for silence and aimed his various piles of hair at me.

"Mr. Haspenhausen is not a firstborn son; therefore, the question is out of order. Good day, Sir."

I should have left it alone, but I knew Aunt Hypatia would acquire all of the details of this meeting and I couldn't give her grounds for reproach.

"Yes, that is normally an obstacle, but apparently there's this thingy in the constitution that gives the heir of Percy Chippington-Smythe—that's me—a bit of leeway."

The committee turned to stare at a member at one end of the table whom I knew to be the parliamentarian. He shrank under their gaze.

"I'm afraid that's true... technically."

"Well, is it true or not?" demanded the Committee Head.

The parliamentarian hemmed and hawed a bit. "Well... it's true."

There was another round of cats being boiled before the Head restored order.

"He may have the power to propose, but we still must vote on the matter. All those in favour of admitting Caspar the Delinquent Ghost as a member of Twits, say aye."

There was a deafening silence. I breathed a sigh of relief.

"And all those opposed..."

At that moment there was a knock on the door. Mr. Nosegurgle opened it to admit... my Uncle Hugo! No one was more surprised than I. He raised a hand diffidently.

"Terribly sorry to interrupt, but I assume you are in the process of voting down my nephew Caspar's application for membership?"

"We are," replied the Head.

"Then on his behalf I claim the right of Trial by Ordeal."

Well, if the previous outbursts had reminded one of roasting cats, this new bombshell caused a furor that must have sounded like one of those things they used to call "zoos" in which any number of bygone beasts used to bellow and roar.

The Head pounded for order. "Don't you understand what this means? If you open the membership to a trial by ordeal then anyone can take up the challenge! We shall be flooded with the dregs of society. There's no telling what sort of reprehensible aspirant may win, and once he's a member so are his firstborn descendants until the end of time. You are opening Pandora's Box!"

My uncle was unperturbed. "Nevertheless," he said.

The Head turned to the parliamentarian. "Are we bound to comply with this outrageous demand?"

The parliamentarian was leafing quickly through an enormous document. He jabbed a finger at one paragraph and muttered to himself, then jabbed at another. Finally, he put down the document and looked up. "I'm afraid there is no way out. A trial by ordeal must be conducted. The winner must be awarded membership."

The committee looked shell-shocked and I must say I felt a bit wobbly myself. I saw at once that this had been Aunt Hypatia's plan from the start. I had been her cat's-paw and my uncle had delivered the fatal blow. If Caspar won the ordeal, then nothing on earth could keep his braying laugh from echoing through the hallowed halls of Twits until grim death should take us all into his icy embrace.

CHAPTER THREE

The Ruptured Spleen

I'm sure you've heard that old saw, "No good deed goes unpunished." I had tried to do my aunt a solid and it had bitten me rather painfully in the tender parts. As I exited the conference room, Uncle Hugo seized my arm in an iron grip and steered me around a corner into an alcove. He shoved his perspiring face close to mine and glared into my eyes feverishly.

"Now, you listen to me, you inbred remnant of a once-noble line. If that blasted nephew of mine succeeds in gaining membership, I shall make it the work of my remaining years to see your life blighted and your reputation shattered. Do I make myself clear?"

I gazed at him in astonishment. "But Uncle, you're the one who brought up the trial by ordeal! The committee would have voted him down in a moment."

"I did what I had to do. Your aunt would have made my life a living hell had I refused, but Caspar must not succeed at the ordeal. He must fail and his failure must not be traced back to me. Do you understand?"

"I must say, this feels rather unfair."

"If life were fair there would be no such things as marriage or dance recitals. You've been far too sheltered. A little adversity will be good for you. Now step outside. Your aunt is waiting on the street to speak with you."

I resignedly trudged out through the lobby and found my aunt sitting in the back of her car. She rolled down the window and beckoned to me with a manicured claw.

"Is it settled? There will be a trial by ordeal?"

"Yes. Everything went off just as you planned it. I must say, you could have told me what you were up to. I had rather an excess of egg on my face."

"History has shown that the less you know the better. That is true of most young people, which is why I have always opposed public education."

"They are sure to make the ordeal as difficult as possible. Caspar is most unlikely to win."

"That would be true if he were forced to compete using only his native abilities which are shockingly feeble, but fortunately for him I am assigning you the task of seeing to it that he succeeds."

I goggled at her. "Me? How on earth do you propose that I do that?"

She looked away. "I will not inquire into how you do it, but you must discover what the test will be and prepare Caspar accordingly. You had better inform me as well. I may have some salient thoughts."

"What a beastly morning this has been! Why did it have to happen on the one day when Bentley is missing in action?"

"You rely entirely too much on Bentley. You possess resources of your own. Gird your feeble loins and do what must be done. Your cousin Caspar is waiting for you at The Ruptured Spleen."

She tinkled a little bell and the car glided away from the curb. I am unaccustomed to feeling more than one emotion at a time, so the riot of conflicting loyalties and opposing directives within my brain rather paralyzed me. I stood on the sidewalk, letting the chants of the protesters who were always to be found outside of Twits wash over me. They seemed particularly insistent today that the rich pay a higher percentage of taxes. This seemed unrealistic to me as, to my certain knowledge, the rich pay no taxes at all and twice nothing is nothing—even three or four times nothing is nothing. That is arithmetic and therefore unassailable.

I jumped as a finger tapped me on the shoulder. Binky was watching me carefully with a worried look on his pasty mug.

"Are you all right? What in heaven's name is going on? The club is buzzing like a hive of mechanical bees."

I heaved a sigh. "I am not all right. I may never be all right again." I proceeded to lay out before him the opposing forces that were crushing me in the teeth of their narrowing jaws.

He gave a low whistle. "That's hard cheese, Old Hatchet. What are you going to do?"

I considered for a moment. "The most formidable of the parties is my aunt, without question. I shall begin by trying to gain any advantage I can for Caspar. With luck, Bentley will be back before further action is needed. If anyone can crack this nut, it is he."

Binky screwed up his face to indicate deep thought. "The ordeal will be devised by the Club Marshall. Cubby is certain to come up with something nasty."

"Perhaps he'll let something slip. You nose around here while I see if Caspar is sober."

"Not much chance of that."

"It's early in the day. He may be in that sentient period between last night's hangover and today's bender. I'll meet you back here after lunch."

The Ruptured Spleen is only a block from Twits, but it might as well be in another world. No brass and Naugahyde here—it had been cobbled together from packing crates and plastic tarpaulins. The bartender was barely humanoid and the spirits it served tasted more medicinal than artisanal. This establishment had two irresistible attractions for a character like Caspar—it was cheap and one could run a tab. He was usually to be found in the center of the room holding court before a collection of disgraced scions and aspiring criminals. Today was no exception. Caspar wore a painfully bright ensemble. A tall, dome-shaped policeman's hat sat incongruously on his pumpkin-shaped head. His puffy face was flushed and sweaty and he held a tall glass of some murky liquid that he sipped between brays. He had assembled a tower of chairs at least ten feet tall and stood beside it like a carnival barker.

"Everyone clear on the bet? If I can climb into the top chair and finish my drink before it all collapses then I win. Right!"

He wedged one foot into the stack and grasped for a hold with his free hand. Of course, as soon as he gave the first pull everything came tumbling down on top of him with a crash! Caspar struggled to his feet and regarded the pile of furniture much as I imagine Caesar regarded Brutus and his shiv. Suddenly he caught sight of me and his face brightened like a child with a stick who spies a piñata.

"Cyril! Say, chaps, it's my cousin Cyril. He'll settle up." He muttered out of the side of his mouth, "Do me a solid and pay these fellows off, will you? It's pocket change to you."

"Pleased, I'm sure," said I, peeling off the required bills and shoving them into the procession of greasy palms that approached me. "Listen, Caspar, could I have a little word?"

He waved dismissively at his entourage. "Shove off, fellows. I've got to have a chin wag with my rich, successful ass of a cousin."

"Now really," I winced.

He let out his trademarked bray. "I'm only pulling your nose, Chippy."

"Please don't call me that. No one has called me Chippy since I was eight."

"You shall always be Chippy to me, Cousin. The name brings back so many happy memories."

I flipped through a selection of the memories he must have been referring to: Caspar pushing my face into a mud puddle under the gaze of my childhood crush; Caspar tripping me on the dais on my way to receive the prize for poetry recitation; Caspar hiding vodka in my trunk on inspection day.

My tormentor straightened the policeman's bonnet that had slid over one ear.

"One hesitates to inquire, but how do you come to be wearing a policeman's hat? Have you joined the constabulary?"

He leered at me. "You know me better than that. I was enjoying a little tipple on the upper deck of the Piccadilly omnibus and saw this fellow waving his arms like a semaphore so I leaned over and nipped his hat. Just a bit of fun."

"You won't think it's much fun when they toss you in the pokey."

"You're such a stick, Chippy. I don't know why you don't hang yourself."

This sort of badinage was getting us nowhere. "Look here, what's all this about you wanting to be a member of Twits?"

He looked glum. "Fat chance of that. Those walruses will never let me in. It was our aunt's idea, really. I wouldn't have wasted my time."

This was a promising start. "You don't have to go through with it. I could call it off."

He straightened up and glared at me. "No you don't! It might not have been my idea but I'm not going to slink away on my belly. I wouldn't give those toffee noses the satisfaction. Besides, if I do get in, I'll be immune from prosecution. I could nab policemen's hats to my heart's content and no one could touch me."

"That is not what membership in Twits is for," I responded rather icily. "As a member you would be expected to uphold the good name of the club by hewing to the highest of moral standards."

He barked a laugh. "Do you hear yourself? That club is the refuge of the most heinous criminals going. Calling them robber barons would be a compliment!"

I stiffened. "I resent your characterization. I have observed only the purest ethical behavior from my fellow members."

He studied me closely. "I believe you mean it. You really are one of heaven's simple fools, Chippy."

I sighed deeply. "I didn't come here to fight. Do you or do you not wish to go through with the trial by ordeal?"

"I do. Damn the torpedoes. I'll give it the old college try."

"Fine. Our aunt has ordered me to prepare you as best I can."

"That seems like the blind leading the drunk. How do you propose to do it?"

I considered. Perhaps it was best not to let him in on the dirty dealings that were underway. He had a low enough opinion of the morals of club members. "The first thing is, you've got to stop drinking at once. Not another drop until the ordeal is over."

"Absolutely not. What else?"

"I... hmm... perhaps you should get some exercise. Go for a hike or a swim. Breathe deeply." I wracked my brain trying to remember the advice I had been given over the years. "Eat large quantities of pasta."

"That I can do. I know you mean well, Chippy, but I think I'm better off just showing up in my usual state of mild inebriation. Anything else would be a shock to my system."

"Fine. Come by the house tonight and we'll put Bentley on the case. Where are you lodging now?"

"Here. They let me sleep it off in the storage room."

"I say, that's beastly. I could put you up in a hotel."

"You're a good egg, Chippy, but I like it here. I'm only a few steps away from everything I need. Why don't you just give me the cash you would have spent on a hotel? Much more convenient."

I grimly peeled more bills out of my wallet and handed them over. "You'll be hearing from me soon."

"Righto. Don't let the door hit you on the way out."

"And give that hat back to the policeman you took it from before you get into trouble."

"Can't do it. Don't know his name. Can't go riding the bus all over town looking for a copper with no hat. Waste of time. I'll just hold on to it."

I trudged grimly back toward the club. Deep
in thought, I didn't spy the approaching danger
until I had almost trod on the patent leather
heels of my nemesis—Cubby Martinez, the
supercilious Marshall of Twits. He was deep
in conversation with his stepsister, Euphonia
Gumboot. I had found myself in more than one
sticky situation involving Euphonia. She was in
the unfortunate position of lacking a short-term
memory. This forced one to re-introduce oneself
to her at every encounter and had led to
numerous misunderstandings until she devised
the expedient of taking meticulous notes in a
small pad which hung around her neck on a cord.
Now, when there was a misunderstanding caused
by her lack of recollection, she had merely to
page through her notes to remind herself of the
event in question. I could see her scribbling as
Cubby talked to her intently. He accompanied
his recitation with copious gestures and I was
somewhat discomfited to see an actual smile on
his face. It gave him a rather gruesome aspect and
I was forced to look away.

I slowly rotated and was just oiling into the crowd to escape them when Euphonia spotted me. She let out a bray. "What a funny-looking gentleman! Cubby, do I know that man? Something about his face makes me shiver in the most delicious manner. Is he a famous murderer? Or perhaps he and I were engaged in a passionate affair? I can look him up alphabetically if you tell me his name."

Cubby glared at me grimly. "He is Cyril Chippington-Smythe. You have been acquainted but your associations with him have led to nothing but unhappiness. Please don't let us detain you, Mr. Chippington-Smythe. You obviously have somewhere to be."

Euphonia was leafing through her book. "Here you are!" She read for a moment. "Goodness, it seems our past meetings have been tumultuous. According to my notes I considered marrying you at one time. I see no footnote indicating the outcome. Were we wed?"

I cleared my throat nervously. "Um, no, you decided that we'd better call it a day. You were far too good for a hound like me."

She began scribbling. "But I shall certainly record our latest meeting. It is pleasant to meet with former beaus, especially when one has spurned them. It makes one feel superior which is very satisfying. Have you suffered terribly since I turned you away?"

"Er, well... at first, of course... but I managed to salve my wounded pride and go on with what was left of my life."

Cubby was watching this interchange with a sneer on his face. "That is quite enough, Euphonia. I must return to the club. Enterprises of great pith and moment are afoot."

I perked up. "That would be the Trial by Ordeal, wouldn't it Cubby? What have you got planned?"

"Nothing that you need to know about, Chippington-Smythe. You'd spread it all over the club by tea time."

Euphonia was reading her notebook. "It's going to be great fun, though. Cubby does this sort of thing so well."

Cubby took the pad from her hands and closed it. "Not another word, Euphonia. I'll see you this evening. Can you find your way home?"

"Oh yes. I've tied little red ribbons along the route. It works admirably except on Saint Valentine's Day when everyone tends to put out red ribbons. I wandered around endlessly one Valentine's Day so now I just stay home until

Mardi Gras. Good day, Mr... whatever your name is."

With that, Euphonia wheeled around and surveyed the square. Spotting a red ribbon tied to a fence she cried, "Tallyho! I'm off."

Cubby sniffed in my direction and made a beeline for the club. I stood for a moment feeling a wave of impotence sweep through me, then hung my head and plodded into the lobby. I was no closer to discovering the secrets of the coming ordeal and I had no idea how to proceed. Bentley would not return until the evening and I was thrown onto my own resources—a perilous place to be.

I entered the bar to find Binky sipping a Naughty Vicar—the club drink. I moped over to him and flopped onto a stool.

He regarded me thoughtfully. "You look as if you'd been run over, tied in a sack and dropped in the river."

I motioned to Sven, the bartender, to bring me one of the same. My stomach reminded me that I had eaten nothing all morning. I reached for a bowl of crackers on the bar and began to shovel them in. Binky reached for the bowl but I slapped his hand away. "Have you discovered anything?"

He shook his head mournfully. "Not a peep. Cubby's keeping this one close to the vest."

"All is lost," I solemnly intoned. I recounted the horrors of the morning to him as Sven set down my drink.

A Naughty Vicar is the king of beverages. Composed of multiple layers of various spirits and juices that lay atop each other like the pages of a book, it is creamy, spicy and sweet. It elevates one's mood and sharpens one's wits. The secret of its recipe was known only to Sven, who guarded it like the crown jewel it was.

Binky frowned. "You say Cubby was talking to Euphonia?"

"Yes. What of it?"

"He seemed excited, you say? He actually smiled?"

"It was horrible. I shall never be able to unsee it."

"I'll bet you anything you like that he was telling her about the ordeal! You know how conceited Cubby is. He'd be bursting to tell someone how clever he is and there's no one at the club he can confide in."

I sat up straight. "If he told Euphonia, she'd write it down in her book!"

"Exactly."

"You know how difficult it is to get it away from her. Last time I had to jump in a river."

Binky looked thoughtful. "You came upon them as he was telling her his plan?"

"I did."

"And she wrote your encounter up directly after?"

"She did."

"Then you must get her to look up what she wrote about you and somehow contrive to get her to tell you what is in the entry directly before it."

"I don't even know where she lives."

"Did you see which way she was walking? Perhaps you can catch her."

I jumped from my stool. "Of course! She was following a trail of red ribbons. They will lead me right to her!" I tossed down the last of my Naughty Vicar. "Wish me luck, Old Wrench."

"*Bonne Chance,*" chirped Binky, raising his glass in salute.

I raced out to the square and spied the first red ribbon at the entrance to Pig Tussle Lane. Trotting along at a steady clip I spotted ribbon after ribbon until, turning a corner into Emphysema Alley I spotted Euphonia looking dreamily into the window of a tea shop. I pulled up next to her and gazed at the scene within. I considered how to break into her reverie without casting her into a fugue state when she turned to me as if we were in the middle of a long conversation.

"Were you going to invite me to tea, Mr. Chippington-Smythe?" She asked gravely.

"As a matter of fact," I stammered, "I was."

CHAPTER FOUR

A Bit of Sleuthing

There is something immensely comforting about a tea shop. Sounds are muted by the immense quantities of chintz on every surface. Customers sit in a carbohydrate-induced stupor. There is the clink of silverware on china and the delightful smell of oleo-margarine and glucose. Euphonia and I slid into a table by the window and a waiter materialized at once. It was a comforting old jalopy of a thing, with a gray wig slightly askew on its shiny dome.

"Tea for two?" it inquired.

"Two for tea," I agreed.

"What kinds of sandwiches do you have?" Euphonia asked eagerly.

"Newcumber, Unimaginable Ham, Fanciful Salmon and Preposterous Cress."

"We'll have the lot... and cake."

"Very good, Miss." It rolled away and we regarded each other speculatively.

"I say, Euphonia, that was a bit of a surprise—you remembering my name just now."

"Did I? What was it?"

"Chippington-Smythe."

"Who's that?"

"Me. I'm Cyril Chippington-Smythe."

"Well, you needn't sound so proud of it."

"I'm not. It's just my name."

"What is?"

"Cyril... never mind. Here's our tea."

Our server deposited a silvery tower covered with finger sandwiches and pastries in the center of the table and arranged the teapot with its accouterments before us.

I lifted the pot. "Shall I be mother?"

"I don't think you're biologically equipped but I shall defend to the death your right to try."

"I mean, shall I pour the tea?"

"If you like."

I busied myself pouring tea and juggling creamer and sugar. We sipped in silence. I madly tried to think of a way to introduce the subject of her notebook.

"That was a bit of serendipity, running into each other by the club earlier, what?"

"Did we?"

"Yes indeed. It was quite an interesting meeting, don't you think?"

Euphonia gave no sign that she had heard me. She was greedily piling sandwiches onto her plate.

"It was so interesting that I believe you made a note of it in your little journal."

"These Preposterous Cress sandwiches are lovely. Do try one."

"You wrote for quite a while. I remember wondering what on earth you could be writing... in that pad of yours."

She stopped chewing and stared at me.

"You are Mr. Chippington-Smythe."

"Indeed I am."

"It is unusual for me to remember someone without looking them up first. You must have made a powerful impression on me."

"Perhaps you should see what you wrote about me... in your book."

At last, she reached for the notebook that hung around her neck. She turned to the most recent entry and smoothed the page with her fingers.

"Oh dear, I've gotten oleo-margarine all over it." She tried to wipe it clean. "Now I've smeared it. How unfortunate. I can't read this very well." She peered at her writing. "Something about an old beau still pining away." She looked up. "Is that you, Mr. Chippington-Smythe? Are you pining away for me?"

I bounced nervously in my chair. "Er... I think that was another chap. Perhaps the bit about me is a little further up the page? Can you read that?"

She moved her finger up and labouriously tried to decipher the smeared writing. "I don't think this is you. It is all about langoustines."

"Langoustines? Are you sure?"

"That's what it looks like." She murmured softly as she read. "The langoustine challenge. Success is inconceivable."

I slid my chair forward with a squeal. "Is there any more? Perhaps it mentions me a little further up?"

She continued deciphering the smeared writing. "Something about cats... or oats... no, I believe it's cats." She looked up at me. "Do you have a cat, Mr. Chippington-Smythe?"

"No. Alas."

"Then this can't be about you." I'm afraid that's all there is. This cake is excellent."

The rest of the tea passed in a blur. I was vibrating with excitement trying to make sense of the clues I had discovered. At last, Euphonia set down her cup with a sigh. The waiter quickly cleared the table.

"Thank you for a lovely tea, Mr. Langoustine."

"Chippington-Smythe."

"Why did I think it was Langoustine?"

"We spoke of them earlier."

"At any rate, I have quite forgiven you for whatever caused me to reject your suit in younger days. You may call on me if you like."

"How good of you. I'm afraid... er... that I'm going on quite a long voyage... may not be back for some time... wouldn't dream of asking you to wait for me. Best to get on with your life and leave me in the dust where I belong."

"I believe you do yourself an injustice, but as you wish." She surveyed the newly cleaned tablecloth. "Have we had our tea? I'm afraid I'm not very hungry. Perhaps we should come back another day when I have more of an appetite."

"Yes. That's probably best. I really should be getting back to the club."

I ushered Euphonia out of the shop, pointed her at the next red ribbon and raced back to tell Binky what I had discovered.

I stopped at the entryway to the club and mopped my sweating brow. Moving quickly was frowned upon in the halls of Twits. I paced through the lobby and headed for the bar. As I plodded down the hallway past Cubby's office, the door slammed open and Cheeseworth flew into the hall, followed by his social media team. He straightened his disordered clothing and shook his fist at the closed door.

"Never in my life have I been tweated so shamefully! The committee shall hear of this!"

The sketch artist recovered his pad from the carpet, spied me and began sketching me with lightning speed. The gentleman with the bag-covered vest scribbled hastily on a strip of paper.

"Cubby Martinez to face disciplinary action! Trashbag, Bad Marshall!" He stuffed the strip of paper in one of his tiny bags and stood staring at me appraisingly.

"I say, Cheeseworth, what's all this about? Have you bearded Cubby in his lair? What's got him in such an uproar?"

Cheeseworth had recovered his sangfroid. He popped a jeweled monocle into one eye and smiled grimly. "I only wished to complain about the attendant in the lavatory. I suspected him of spying on me but I couldn't be certain. I offered to pay him for the service but he wefused. Appawently doing it for money takes the fun out of peeping. I came to ask Cubby to insist on his compliance but he's obsessed with the upcoming ordeal and when I discovered him plotting and planning on his little chalkboard, he shrieked like a steam whistle and thwew me out."

Something like hope rose up within me. "Did you see what was on the chalkboard? Can you tell me what it said?"

He waved a hand airily. "No idea, my boy. I was too busy being given the bum's rush to take much notice."

The rising hope within me drank arsenic. "Oh well, it would have been too good to be true."

The sketch artist tore the top page from his pad and held it up for inspection. He was getting the knack of my nose, but I felt sure that I possessed more chin than was evident in the drawing. Suddenly I stared at the page that had lain under my likeness. It was a sketch of Cubby's office. I seized the pad over the objections of its owner and stared at it. In the center of the sketch was a chalkboard and on it one could just make out the words "Carrot Challenge." I whooped and threw a fist in the air. The sketch artist grabbed his pad and smoothed its pages sulkily.

Cheeseworth watched all this curiously. "I didn't know you were such a devotee of art, dear boy."

"I haven't been up to now, Cheeseworth, but I am beginning to grasp how much one can learn from it if one looks hard enough!"

I raced into the bar to find Binky in the midst of a conga line between our old pals Ford and Lincoln.

"Hallo, Old Badger," trumpeted Ford. "Hook on! It's marvelous exercise. Takes the place of any number of jumping jacks."

"It's all in the hips," Lincoln agreed. "It beats the Hully-Gully all hollow."

I stamped a foot. "This is no time for the conga. Our world is crumbling about our ears!"

They ground to a halt and regarded me sympathetically.

"Poor fellow," murmured Ford.

Lincoln pounded my shoulder with what I'm sure was meant to be sympathy. "Binky has told us everything. Nominated Caspar the Delinquent Ghost, did you? There will be any number of towels snapping at your genitals in the locker room, Old Colostomy bag."

I gave Binky a withering look. "It was meant to be a secret."

He dug a toe into the carpet. "But surely not from our friends."

Ford slapped a thick hand on my rump causing me to jump. "Don't blame Binky, we winkled it out of him."

"Blame the Naughty Vicars," hooted Lincoln.

"Look, fellows, give us a little privacy, won't you? We'll call you if any muscle work is needed." Binky managed to shoo the pair away. I dragged him into a corner and revealed the fruits of my endeavors.

"Carrots? What could the test possibly be? Cooking them? Eating them? It makes no sense. And langoustines... I don't see how this intelligence gets us any closer to helping Caspar to pass the ordeal."

"You just wait. Bentley will be back soon and he'll untangle it all. I need you to collect the Delinquent Ghost at the Ruptured Spleen and bring him to my house after dinner. I'm going to send a message to my aunt." I frowned grimly. "It's time to convene for a war council."

CHAPTER FIVE

The Candidate Prepares

After the beastly day I had endured, the sight of the ancestral manse was like a balm. I hurried up to the front door, which was opened immediately by... Bentley! Words cannot express my relief. He shone with paste wax and brilliantine.

"Good evening, Sir. Welcome home."

"Oh, Bentley, thank heavens you're back! We're in a bit of a cocked hat I'm afraid."

"Indeed, Sir, I have learned of the developments that have occurred since my departure. A most perilous situation, if I may say."

"You may and it is. Thankfully I have resources of my own and with a herculean effort I have managed to discover invaluable clues that will reveal the tests that Cubby has devised for the ordeal. The first has something to do with carrots and in the second the candidates will be tested on their knowledge of langoustines. There is a mysterious odor of cats lingering over it all."

Bentley gave a quiet sigh. "Yes, Sir, I have all the necessary details."

I gawped at him. "Do you? How?"

"Human beings have a tendency to regard mechanical servants as invisible. While a member of the club could not enter Mr. Martinez's office with impunity, a cleaning robot can come and go without notice. I simply asked the club custodian to retrieve the contents of Mr. Martinez's waste basket."

"You mean I practically killed myself to get this information and you already knew it?"

"I'm sure it was an invigorating exercise, Sir."

"But what are the tests? What does 'carrots' imply? Why this obsession with sea creatures?"

The doorbell sang out with "Lady of Spain."

Bentley paced toward the door. "I shall reveal all when the company is assembled, Sir."

He opened the door to reveal Binky and Caspar, who was reeling just a bit.

"Let the games begin," he roared, and fell face-first into the hallway.

Bentley picked him up and misted off to prepare one of his eye-openers.

Binky regarded Caspar critically. "Not a good beginning, I'm afraid."

"Lady of Spain" rang out again and the door opened to reveal Aunt Hypatia. She strode into the front hallway. "Well, Nephew, have you done as I asked?"

"As it happens, I have. The secrets of the ordeal lie before us like an open book. We're just about to begin Caspar's preparation."

"Good. I shall observe and offer what advice I can."

We gathered in my study, where Bentley had laid out a selection of apparel. It was rather pleasant to see so many of my triumphant ensembles cheek by jowl. On a table in the center of the room lay a variety of neckwear in every conceivable colour and pattern. I spotted several items which had led to sharp disagreements between Bentley and myself.

Binky was in heaven. He rushed from one outfit to the next cooing and feeling the fabrics with a covetous gleam in his eye. "Marvelous! Give me

Bentley and a line of credit with the tailor and I would set the fashion world on its ear."

Caspar slumped in a chair regarding the proceedings with a jaundiced eye. "What's it all about, Chippy? Why am I staring at your old clothes? Is the challenge to construct a raft with them and sail to the South Seas?"

Bentley stepped to the front of the room and cleared his throat. "We are assembled here to prepare Mr. Haspenhausen for the coming ordeal. The test has two parts. The first challenge is one of fashion. It is devious, difficult and will undoubtedly eliminate most of the challengers."

I raised a hand. "I don't see what this has to do with carrots, Bentley."

"I'm afraid that Mr. Cheeseworth's sketch artist is not a man of fashion. The word on Mr. Martinez's chalkboard was not 'carrot,' Sir, it was 'cravat.' This is a cravat challenge."

Binky gave a shiver. "It's delicious! I almost wish I was competing. I'm a sort of idiot savant when it comes to clothing, you know."

"Yes, I'm well aware." I squinted at the cravats on the table. "How does it work?"

Bentley picked up one of my favourites—a lime green number with orange stripes. "It is meant to judge one's taste, Sir. The challenge is to match the proper cravat with any ensemble the judge cares to name."

"That doesn't seem too hard. The one in your hand would go with any of these."

"No, Sir, that is incorrect. In actual fact, it is unsuitable for any article of clothing. To choose it would mean instant elimination."

I smiled at Bentley condescendingly. "I am aware that our tastes diverge on occasion, but I think you are being overly censorious."

"On the contrary. We have never spoken of the laws of cravats, Sir, but I assure you that there is a system which rivals the Code of Hammurabi. It is known to all domestic servants. I have taken the liberty of creating a chart."

Bentley unrolled a sheet of parchment roughly the size of a tablecloth and fastened it to the wall with a few thumb tacks. We all walked over to stare at it. Along one side was a rainbow of cravats. Across the top of the chart was a list of items of apparel in various colours. A complex web of lines led from cravat to outfit. There were shaded bars that seemed to indicate times of year and major holidays and a large section of footnotes that listed various exceptions based on capricious ephemera like "When in mourning, substitute 12E for 5M" or "If fish is being served, eliminate all shades from yellow through red."

Binky ran to the chart and stared. "I have heard rumours of this system but I thought it was only a myth, like sea serpents or free checking."

Just looking at it made my head ache. "This is impossible! No one could possibly learn all of this."

My aunt was peering at the chart intently. "Most interesting. I shall take possession of this paper when Caspar is through with it. Hugo's days of whimsical neckwear are at an end."

Bentley swept an arm toward the chart. "This system has its scientific basis in how colour affects the human nervous system. Applied correctly, the colour combinations set forth here can influence the observer on a chemical level to produce feelings of goodwill, romance or envy as desired. Misuse of the system can lead to feelings of aggression or, in extreme cases, nausea."

"It's incredible!" I turned resignedly to Caspar, who was still slumped in his chair. "I don't suppose you know anything about all this?"

He lurched to his feet and staggered to the chart. He focused his eyes on it for a moment and fell back into his chair. "Got it," he belched.

I stared at him. "What do you mean, 'got it'? Got what?"

He jabbed his forefinger at his forehead. "Eidetic memory. I can't forget anything I read. It's one of the reasons I drink. Only way to shut it all off."

We all regarded him with astonishment.

"You remember everything you've ever read?" I stammered.

"Everything. Every book, every menu, every laundry bill. They swim before my eyes at night like vengeful ghosts. I haven't slept soundly in years."

"Poor chap! Can no one help?"

"No one. Doctors are all quacks. Tell me to surround myself with nature and avoid the printed word. Good luck with that. We're assaulted with advertisements every waking moment. I can quote every product slogan from Beverly's Beans to Tallywacker's Trusted Trusses."

There you are, you see... just when you think you've got someone pegged as a thorough rotter, they come out with some tragic backstory that makes you empathize with them and you find you can't dislike them no matter how hard you try.

I patted Caspar on the shoulder. "There, there, Old Catapult. Once you're in the club things will look up. There's ever so much fun to be had."

He pushed my hand away. "What you call fun is pure poison to me, Chippy, but let it go. I'll play along. What about the langoustine bit?"

We all turned to Bentley. "The word that Miss Gumboot was trying to decipher through the smear of oleo-margarine was not 'langoustine,' it was 'labyrinth.' The second test will take place in The Labyrinth, Sir."

I should pause here to explain. To the casual observer, Twits is merely another large marble building in a city that was once filled with such edifices. Those initiated into its mysteries soon find that it is a great deal more than that. The builders of Twits discovered that it sat atop an underground cavern that widened as it deepened—forming a kind of pyramid shape that at its base was almost as wide as the city itself. They took advantage of this geological anomaly by building most of Twits underground. The dining room, card room, bar, tea room, etcetera were above ground, but such amenities as the swimming pool, cricket pitch and burial crypts were deep under the city. At the lowest level, placed there for reasons that had been lost to time, was The Labyrinth. Constructed of rough-hewn stones, it was an ancient maze that served no useful purpose that anyone could discern other than as a diversion. Even that was rarely indulged in, as the size and complexity of its convolutions caused many a member to be lost for days at a time and necessitated complex and costly rescue operations. A system of chimneys and mirrors brought air and sunlight down from the surface for illumination. It was rumoured that there was some sort of beast at the center of the maze. This was generally accepted to be a fiction to frighten new members who were often chucked into it after a night of debauchery and left to gibber there in a cul-de-sac until morning.

Bentley continued. "This test is rather diabolical. The aspirant must enter The Labyrinth, locate the club cat, Mrs. Beasely, within it and return her to the entrance by a specified time. It is designed to sound credible, but I believe that Mr. Martinez considers this challenge to be impossible."

"And so it is. No one knows the secrets of The Labyrinth and Mrs. Beasely is the foulest-tempered mammal on the face of the earth. To attempt to remove her would lead to massive blood loss unless one was clad in medieval armor from head to toe."

Caspar shook his head gloomily. "They never wanted anyone to win the challenge. There will be no new member. I knew it was fixed."

Bentley cleared his throat. "I believe I have a solution, Sir."

I was accustomed to Bentley's brainstorms—he is a kind of walking deus ex machina—but this was pretty rich even for him. "Out with it, Bentley. What is it?"

"I believe that the answer to our conundrum is cat food."

I eyed him suspiciously. "Are you quite all right, Bentley?"

"Never better, Sir."

"And yet you insist that the insurmountable conjunction of destructive forces raining down upon us can be overcome with... cat food?"

His optical sensors vibrated a bit—a phenomenon that I had begun to think was a display of mirth on Bentley's part. "The cornerstone of your misfortunes is the certainty that your cousin will be unable to locate the club cat among the trackless turns of The Labyrinth. I suggest that you precede him into the maze and place a can of cat food at a prearranged location.

The cat, using its superior sense of smell, will seek out the food and your cousin Caspar should easily find Mrs. Beasely enjoying her meal by following the map that you shall give him. If he draws the can of cat food back to the entry by means of a length of cord, the cat will follow without the necessity of physical contact."

My jaw dropped. "By gads, Bentley, what did they do to that brain of yours at the factory? This is one of your masterstrokes!"

"You overestimate my abilities as usual, Sir."

My aunt rose from her seat. "Well done, Nephew. I will leave you to consider all the possible contingencies that may arise and to practice until Caspar is as prepared as possible. We shall see each other tomorrow at the signing-in ceremony of the trial by ordeal." She retrieved the chart that Bentley had made for the cravat challenge. "You will not need this, since its details are already contained within Caspar's memory. Good night to you all."

She swept out the door. I looked around at our little band of conspirators. "All right, everyone, let us begin."

There followed an intensive session on cravats, which Caspar passed easily thanks to his faultless memory. We huddled around the table and carefully drew up two copies of the map which would lead Caspar and me to the spot in The Labyrinth where I would place the cat food.

Binky looked skeptical. "How do you know this map matches the actual maze?"

"It doesn't matter. It's just a series of turns—right, right, left, left and so on. The important thing is that our maps match. Then it's just a matter of following it in reverse to get back to the entrance."

At last, Bentley began clearing away the assembled clothing. "I believe that Mr. Haspenhausen is as prepared as it is possible to be," he said. "A good night's sleep is the best course of action at this point."

We stood around the table and looked at each other. Our little band of brothers was about to be sorely tested by the evil designs of Cubby Martinez.

"Victory or death," I declared.

Caspar snorted. "You can die if you want to, Chippy. I'm not going to commit self-slaughter if they don't let me into their little club." He must have seen my head droop, for his tone grew softer. "I do appreciate all the trouble you've taken. Perhaps you're not the chancre sore I took you for."

I brightened at once. "That's all right. It's a common misperception."

"Don't be too disappointed if I muff it."

Just do your best. No one can ask more than that."

He headed for the drinks cart. "How about a Naughty Vicar to celebrate?"

Binky raised an eyebrow. "That would be super, but only Sven knows the secret recipe."

Caspar was tossing this and that into shakers and pitchers. "No one but Sven and I. I tasted a Naughty Vicar once and was able to recreate it from memory."

"Impossible!" I gasped.

"You'll see." He arranged three glasses and then proceeded to pour the contents of pitchers and shakers over the back of a spoon in alternating layers. When he was finished, something that looked very much like three Naughty Vicars sat before us.

Binky picked his up and held it to the light. "It certainly looks right, but the proof is in the drinking."

We all picked up our drinks. "Down the hatch, boys," said Caspar.

We sipped. We sipped again. It was unquestionably a Naughty Vicar!

"Astonishing!" sighed Binky. "Can you teach it to me?"

Caspar nodded. "It's the least I can do."

He arranged bottles and glasses and we all huddled over them in the lamplight like three wizened alchemists who have discovered the secret of turning lead into gold.

CHAPTER SIX

The First Test

The day of the contest was suitably grim. A cold sprinkle of rain found its way into gaps in collars and shoes. A large tent had been set up in front of the club so that the non-members could be kept outside until the test began. Bentley had accompanied me to hold an umbrella. We ducked under the canvas flap to behold a seething mass of humanity shoving and crying out as Cubby and his helpers tried desperately to form them into lines.

I spied several younger brothers of club members. There was Badger Binghampton's brother, Budgie, and I spotted Spigot Huffnagle's youngest sibling, Plum-Bob, trying to cut in line.

I felt a tap on my shoulder and turned to find a familiar beaming face.

"What a pleasure to see you again, Sir," boomed Ahmed Ben-Fitzwilliam.

I had last seen the former club hatter of Twits in the Northern Wilderness, where he had taken employment as the leader of a chicken-worshiping cult. "What on earth brings you to town, Mr. Fitzwilliam? Won't your followers be missing you?"

"Most assuredly they will," he assured me with a chuckle, "But when news reached me of the trial by ordeal, I could not let the chance to become a member of Twits pass me by."

"No, indeed, I quite understand. Best of luck to you."

"Thank you, Sir. I shall do my utmost."

He scuttled back into line and I leaned toward Bentley. "He's sure to pass the cravat test. After all, fashion is his profession."

Bentley shook his head. "Mr. Fitzwilliam will not pass the test. He possesses an Achilles heel that will cause his downfall."

"Does he? What is this defect in his character?"

"Mr. Fitzwilliam believes that he has taste, Sir. Consequently, he will not make the scientific choice. He will wish to make a statement and this will be his undoing."

I spotted another familiar face entering the tent. "Ernie! Are you entering the ordeal?"

Ernie was the head of research at Smythe Corporation. He was a certified genius and there was certainly no possibility of Caspar out-thinking him.

"I am, Sir. It was Mum's idea. I'm infiltrating the bastion of capitalist oppression or something of that nature."

Ernie's Mum was my cook who, coincidentally, was named Cook. She was a culinary phenomenon as well as a confirmed socialist.

"Best of luck to you, Ernie."

"Thank you, Sir. Do you know what the test will be? I hope we don't have to eat anything nasty."

I blushed at having to deceive him. "I have no idea, but I'm sure you'll do splendidly."

Caspar was pushing his way into the tent. He had clearly fortified himself with copious quantities of alcohol. He reeled in my direction.

"Hallo, Chippy. Everything under control?"

"For heaven's sake, couldn't you go easy on the sauce today of all days?"

"Don't scold me. I've got a beastly headache."

"Have you been practicing?"

He winked broadly. "Yes. No worries. I'm primed and ready."

"You'd better get in line. They're almost finished signing the contestants in."

I gave Caspar a gentle shove in the direction of the judges' table as my Aunt Hypatia entered the tent accompanied by a small, gray man carrying a briefcase.

"Hello, Aunt, come to see your protégé off?"

"Not exactly. Excuse me, Nephew, I have business with the committee."

She marched toward the sign-in table and curiosity drew me in her wake. As she reached the table, the last of the contestants finished signing the sheet.

Griffin Scabies, the Committee Head looked up at her. "What may I do for you, Mrs. Dankworth?"

My aunt stood like the figurehead on a battleship. She looked around imperiously. The noise in the tent died to a whisper.

"I wish," She trumpeted, "To enter my name for the trial by ordeal!"

Pandemonium! There was sputtering and choking aplenty. Uncle Hugo, who had been helping out behind the table rushed forward—his face ashen.

"Hypatia! This is no time for levity. Leave this tent at once."

"This is not a joke, Hugo. My solicitor will explain."

The small, gray man pulled some papers out of his briefcase and cleared his throat. "I have studied the charter which created Twits in great detail and have examined in particular the section which lays out the rules for the trial by ordeal. It appears that the founders were so oblivious to the possibility of females wishing to become members that they never bothered to specify that the trial by ordeal was an exclusively male privilege. The document states..." He adjusted his spectacles and peered at the paper in his hand, "Once a trial by ordeal has been declared, any person wishing to enter the challenge shall present themselves before the committee and declare their intention to participate." He looked up. "There is no pronoun used that is either masculine or feminine, therefore my client contends that females are not prohibited from entering."

This set off a firestorm, as you can imagine. The parliamentarian whipped open one book after another and scribbled madly on a notepad. Uncle Hugo, who had taken on a rather blueberry hue, collapsed into a chair and fanned himself with his hat. My aunt opened her purse and took out a large powder puff, with which she methodically powdered herself from hairline to chin.

At last, the parliamentarian threw up his hands. "I'm afraid he is correct. There is nothing in any of the club documents that specifies a sexual requirement to enter the trial by ordeal. She must be allowed to compete."

There was an explosion of objections, which melded into a sort of chorus in which "Razza-razza" seemed to be the only discernible word. After ten minutes or so the din slowly ground to a halt. There was a final, raspy "Razza-razza" from the far end of the tent and then silence. My aunt stepped to the table, picked up the pen and signed her name to the list with a flourish.

Uncle Hugo staggered to his feet. "You have ruined us, Hypatia. We shall be pariahs now."

My aunt snorted. "Don't be a mouse, Hugo. Change does not come through cowardice. Nothing worth accomplishing comes without a price."

I waited until the crowd around my aunt thinned and approached her. "It seems you have played upon me like a fiddle once again, Aunt. You made use of me to prepare you for the tests. Did you ever intend for Caspar to be the winner?"

She looked at me grimly. "Of course not! Your cousin Caspar is like a delicate china bowl in a racing river. He will inevitably be dashed to pieces. He was a means to an end."

"And so was I, apparently."

"But you are made of stronger stuff, although you don't know it yet."

Bentley shimmered up at that point and my aunt gathered herself together. "I must go in. Bentley, thank you for your assistance."

"Good luck, Ma'am, if I may be so forward."

We watched her sail through the front door of Twits—an act that must have sent hundreds of former members spinning in their crypts.

Bentley handed me the furled umbrella. "I may not accompany you inside, but I hope the day unfolds to your satisfaction, Sir."

"Not much chance of that, I'm afraid. I may not be home for dinner, Bentley."

"Very good, Sir."

He slid out of the tent and I girded my loins for what was certain to be a momentously nasty day.

Due to my position as the heir of Percy Chippington-Smythe, I was forced to serve as one of the stewards of the contest. I took my place with the members of the committee behind a long, mahogany table in the billiard room. The gaming tables had been draped with fabric and a large selection of clothing was carefully laid out on top of them.

Cubby addressed us. "As each applicant enters, I shall inform them of the nature of the challenge and of the rules. I shall then choose an ensemble, state the relevant conditions and ask them to match the appropriate cravat to the chosen outfit. Is that clear?"

We nodded our assent and Cubby gestured to the doorkeeper to admit the first victim.

The first challenger was Ahmed Ben Fitzwilliam. The former hatter entered the room with a flourish. He looked eagerly at the clothing laid out on the tables. Cubby rose and explained the rules of the challenge. Fitzwilliam beamed. "Gentlemen," he chortled, "I shall not keep you long. I believe this little test will not be an impediment for one who has devoted his life to fashion."

Cubby referred to a sheet of paper in his hand. He pointed to one of the outfits. "The date is November the twenty-second. The day is sunny. Your second cousin once removed passed away on September the eighth. The dining room is serving spaghetti Bolognese for lunch. Which of these cravats do you choose?"

I watched with interest to see whether Bentley's prediction of his failure would prove accurate. The little man gazed at the selection of cravats. He picked up a plain gray number and smiled at it fondly. Cubby slumped with disappointment. Suddenly, Ahmed Ben Fitzwilliam spied a lavender cravat with jewel-like hummingbirds embroidered on it. I must say, I was drawn to it myself. He picked it up in his other hand and gazed back and forth between the two articles of neckwear. He began to perspire. He held up one cravat to the outfit Cubby had chosen, then the other. He began to make small, mewing sounds. At last, he gave a loud cry and threw the plain gray cravat to the ground.

He held up the hummingbirds in triumph. "It must be this one! It would cause a sensation! I will stake my reputation on it!"

Cubby smiled wolfishly. "I'm afraid that is incorrect, Mr. Fitzwilliam. Bad luck. Please send in the next candidate."

The little hatter slumped with disappointment. "There is the correct choice and there is the artistic choice. I do not regret losing in the name of art."

The next candidate was Ernie. He strolled in and regarded the outfits with interest.

Cubby stepped forward and explained the rules. He indicated an ensemble. "The date is July the fifteenth. The day is cloudy. Which is the proper cravat to match with this ensemble?"

Ernie looked thoughtful. "I suppose the system is based on colour combinations and how their various wavelengths interact. Give me a moment." He drew a pad and a pencil from his pocket and began to calculate. "Blue has a wavelength of... and beige would shorten the curve by... so the cravat should have a wavelength that causes the wave to repeat in a complimentary pattern... in July the sun is at an angle of... clouds would refract by a factor of..."

He finished his calculations and inspected the cravats on the table. He pointed to a buttery yellow bow. "I believe it should be this one."

Cubby's jaw dropped open. "Th-that's correct," he stammered.

Ernie smiled. "Thanks. That was fun. Should I send in the next contestant?"

"Uh, yes, please." Cubby sat down heavily. He wiped his forehead and stared at his sheet. I could see that he was shaken. If Ernie could pass the test, perhaps it wasn't as challenging as he had supposed.

His fears proved unjustified. Applicant after applicant followed Ernie and they all went down in abject defeat.

At last, there were only two challengers left—Aunt Hypatia and Caspar. My aunt swept in and looked down her nose at the assembled judges. She eyed the ensembles laid out on the tables and raised an eyebrow. "Well? What am I to do?"

I had to admire her acting. No one would suppose that she had inside information of the most specific kind.

Cubby ran through the rules and referred to his sheet. "The date is December the twelfth. There is snow on the ground. It is a leap year. You are meeting friends for tea. Which cravat do you choose?"

My aunt looked inward. I knew she was examining a mental picture of the chart that Bentley had created and that she had carried off the night before to study. "The leap year is immaterial. Most people would imagine that because of the snow the proper choice would be this item..." She pointed to a dark blue cravat with light blue stripes... "But we are meeting for tea which will certainly take place among pastels and therefore..." She picked up a lime green item with tiny yellow dots... "This is the item you are looking for."

Cubby slumped with disappointment. "That is correct."

My aunt swept out of the room with a sniff. On her way out the door she caught my eye and gave a tiny smile.

After a moment the door creaked open and Caspar stumbled in. His eyes were bright red and he blew his nose repeatedly into a large, dirty handkerchief.

"Hello, boys," he mumbled. "Got anything to drink?"

Cubby sneered at him. "You can do your drinking after you are eliminated, Mr. Haspenhausen."

He read the rules to Caspar, who stood, swaying and looking about the room.

Cubby pointed to an outfit. "The date is April the first. It is raining. The dining room is serving Fanciful Salmon. Which is the appropriate cravat?"

I stiffened in my seat. I knew that fish on the menu changed the rules. Would Caspar remember?

Caspar reeled a bit. He looked thoughtful for a moment and then laughed. "Nice one, Cubby! The fish was misdirection of course. It's April Fool's Day. You don't wear a cravat at all. You wear a bolo tie."

Cubby looked crushed. I could see that he thought his stroke of genius would mow down the opposition. He feebly dropped his paper on the table. "That is correct."

I pumped my fist under the table. Caspar lived to fight another day!

The committee grumbled a bit. The Head checked his notes. "There seem to be three successful challengers—Mrs. Dankworth, Mr. Haspenhausen and this Ernie person."

Cubby drew himself up. "Do not be alarmed, Gentlemen. The next test will ensure that the halls of Twits will remain unsullied by persons undeserving of the honour."

"Let us hope so," grunted Griffin Scabies.

The committee disbanded to seek refreshment before the next test began. I headed for the bar where I knew Binky would be waiting. He jumped from his stool when he saw me enter.

"How did it go? Did Caspar pass?"

"He did. So did Aunt Hypatia and Ernie."

"Commiserations about your aunt and her machinations, Old Wagon. It doesn't cast a very attractive light on your family tree."

"Don't I know it. I'll never hear the end of it, but I must say I admire the old girl. She's got moxie. There's no denying it."

"She may have moxie, but there is something even more valuable that she doesn't have." He reached into his pocket and slipped out a can of cat food and a can opener. The can had a long coil of fishing line wrapped around it.

"What makes you think she doesn't have her own can of cat food?"

"She may, but she doesn't have you to place it in the maze for her ahead of time. Your uncle would certainly not assist her." He handed over the equipment. "Do you want me to open it for you?"

"No need. Bentley gave me a lesson on opening cans this morning. We'll be eating baked beans for the foreseeable future."

"You'd better toddle on down to The Labyrinth and stow the cat food before the committee shows up."

"Right you are. Wish me luck."

"Of course. Got your map?"

I patted my chest and felt the reassuring crinkle of paper. "All is prepared."

"Off you go then."

I regarded Binky curiously. "I must say, you seem more... competent than usual."

"Am I?"

"One might almost say... helpful."

He considered. "Do you know, my mind does seem clearer. Perhaps it's the Naughty Vicars."

I snapped my fingers. "You haven't mentioned being in love in days. Isn't there some *belle dame sans merci* somewhere gnawing on the old ticker?"

"No. No one."

"That's it, then. All that extra brain space is allowing you some room to spread out. If you stay away from the fairer sex for a while perhaps you could really accomplish something with your life."

He grimaced. "I'm going to the midnight show at the Follies tonight."

"That's that then. I'm off."

I stopped at the door and looked back at the cozy tableau in the bar. A chill of foreboding ran up my spine. I gripped the can of cat food in my pocket and stiffened my back. Generations of diffident Chippington-Smythes had mated to create a genome that bred true for timidity but I would overcome it. Caspar would be victorious and my aunt would be forced to acknowledge that Cyril Chippington-Smythe was a force to be reckoned with.

CHAPTER SEVEN

All is Revealed

I stood at the entrance to the maze and looked around me nervously. Now that the time had come to enter its sinuous pathways, I was feeling rather queer. I had participated in a search party or two over the years. The memories of finding those poor, gibbering initiates with their staring eyes and drooling lips rose up before me—and what of the rumoured beast that haunted the center of The Labyrinth? I shook myself and gripped the can of cat food in my sweating hand. Peering at the map I took a deep breath and stepped across the threshold.

There was just enough dim light filtering in from the vaulted ceiling high overhead to see my way down the passage. At the first fork I carefully turned left. Staring at the map, I made turn after turn: left, right, right, left. I began to feel more confident and picked up the pace a bit: right, right, left. Suddenly I came to a fork where the map told me to turn left, but the only passageway open to me was to my right! I stared at the map, then at the wall. What to do? Retrace my steps? Abandon the plan? I saw no other options. I turned and carefully picked my way back down the passageway. Holding the map upside down I tried to reverse the directions that had brought me here. I was beginning to hear grinding noises that sounded like someone dragging a sack of nails over cobblestones. I was drenched in sweat. At last, I made the final turn and found... another wall! I was lost! The passageways seemed narrower somehow... and darker. I would never find my way out!

I began to run aimlessly, hoping against hope that I would stumble upon the entrance. I turned corner after corner. The grinding noises grew louder. Finally, I was forced to stop by a cramp in my calves. I leaned against the wall and panted for a bit. I considered taking a taste of the cat food to see if it might sustain me when starvation came calling. Fumbling with the opener, I managed to make a jagged rent in the metal can. I stuck a finger in and lifted it to the dim light. A drop of yellow grease hung from the tip. I gagged a bit and wiped the finger on my sleeve.

In the sudden silence I heard a distant gunshot! The test had begun and the three contestants were entering The Labyrinth. I heard faint laughter and hooting from the spectators. A hint of sanity returned and I considered my situation. Caspar was done for—he would never be a Twit. The committee would want to know what I was doing in here with a can of cat food. The rescue party that would eventually find me would have endless fun at my expense.

I wiped away a tiny tear (getting grease in my eye in the process) and straightened my spine. They would not crush my spirit! Cyril Chippington-Smythe was made of sterner stuff. I set off down the passageway at a sedate pace, turned a corner and suddenly staggered into an enormous clearing! The light from the ceiling was directly overhead and illuminated the scene like sunlight. The clearing was filled with plants and flowers. A luxurious lawn surrounded what I could only describe as a lovely, woodland cottage. Smoke rose cheerily from the chimney and roses climbed around the lintel. As I stood staring, the door opened and who should emerge but...

Bentley! I had no time to observe more, for at that point I fainted dead away.

I awoke to find myself sprawled on a brocade sofa with Bentley applying a cool towel dipped in vinegar to my temples. I struggled to sit up.

"What on earth are you doing here, Bentley! What is this place?"

"Remain calm, Sir. All is well. You are in the home of Prissy Chippington-Smythe."

"Who is Prissy Chippington-Smythe? I've never heard of her."

I heard a throat being cleared behind Bentley and as he stepped to the side, I could see an elderly person in a lovely beaded gown sitting in an armchair by the fire. She gazed at me benevolently.

"I am Prissy Chippington-Smythe. Welcome, young Cyril."

I examined her curiously. She certainly had the Chippington-Smythe nose. "I'm most dreadfully embarrassed, but I've never heard of you. In what way are we related?"

The question seemed to discomfit her. She frowned and considered for a moment.

"One fact is indisputable. You are my great-great-grandson."

My head began to swim. "Then you are the widow of Percy Chippington-Smythe, the founder of the family fortune."

She looked at Bentley, then at me. "That is not quite accurate. The fact is that at the time our family achieved its exalted financial position I was known by the name Percy Chippington-Smythe."

I goggled. "But that would make you your own widow."

She gave me an odd look. "Bentley has kept me informed as to your development over the years, but even his reports fell short. I am no one's widow. I realized late in life that my sexual identity was female rather than male and my wealth made it a simple process to correct that error of nature."

This gave me something to chew on, as you can imagine. The change from Percy to Prissy wasn't an insurmountable mental obstacle to overcome. I had more than one friend who had done the same—some in one direction and some in another. Growler Gilhooley who captained the rugby team at university was born Greta. Something else was nagging at me.

"I say, you must be over a hundred years old!"

"I will be one hundred and twenty next March."

I whistled softly. "You don't look it, I must say."

"When one has unlimited wealth the most esoteric of medical procedures are available. Few of my organs are original."

"But Great-great... is it grandfather or grandmother?"

"I suppose it is grandmother, but why not just call me Prissy?"

"But Prissy, why are you hidden away in this maze?"

She gave a little sigh. "It's not so bad, really. I had the cottage built to my specifications and it contains everything I need. Bentley stops by to keep me up to date with the gossip and to bring me books and once a year he does my Spring cleaning."

I eyed Bentley appraisingly. "So you don't go to the factory at all? This yearly tune-up is a ruse?"

He was unperturbed. "I do apologize for the subterfuge. Tune-ups are unnecessary. I do my own maintenance. I have looked after my mistress all of her life and will continue to do so to the best of my abilities... just as I do for you, Sir."

Well, I couldn't complain very hard about that. I turned back to Prissy. "But you should be enjoying the fruits of your labours—kicking up your heels and so on."

She bowed her head pensively. "Alas, it is true that behind every great fortune is a great crime. I committed several financial indiscretions in my youth and the immunity offered by the walls of Twits is the only thing standing between me and prison. It could be argued that I deserve to pay for my crimes, but at my age I would not survive incarceration for long. Besides, my life here, luxurious as the accommodations are, has been a kind of self-imposed prison. I have served many more years than any sentence a judge could have handed down and my guilty conscience has punished me like the mythical furies."

"At least you should have been enjoying the facilities of the club. I've never seen you in the dining room or at the bear baiting pit."

She straightened and her eyes took on a piercing look. "Now we reach the crux of the situation. Twits membership is not open to females and never has been."

This rocked me back on my heels. Of course, she was right. I remembered the case of Spigot Huffnagle, who had similarly decided that he was destined to be a woman and was stripped of his membership by the committee. I had felt rotten about it at the time, but had never thought to question the decision. This cast things in a new light.

"I say, something has got to be done!"

She smiled. "Something *is* being done and your assistance has been invaluable."

"Mine? But I haven't done anything."

At that moment there was a loud knock on the door. Bentley opened it to reveal... my Aunt Hypatia! She strolled into the room as if she was long accustomed to do so and glanced at me approvingly.

"I see you arrived in one piece, Nephew."

"What are you doing here, Aunt?"

"I am winning the trial by ordeal, of course."

She made a clucking noise with her tongue and from some hidden alcove Mrs. Beasely shot into her arMiss My aunt stroked her and made little cooing noises that were quite unlike her.

I stared at them with bewilderment. "How did Mrs. Beasely get here?"

My great-great-grandmother laughed. "Everyone assumes she is the club cat, but she is really my cat. This is her home."

I turned to Bentley a little desperately. "Bentley, an explanation please, before I go thoroughly mad?"

He leaned toward me soothingly. "The explanation is quite simple, Sir. In order for your great-great-grandmother to escape from her solitary exile it was necessary to alter the club rules to allow for the existence of female members. After much study I realized that trial by ordeal was the only way to circumvent the barriers that would certainly be thrown up by the committee... but a trial by ordeal could not be demanded by a female. That would have been dismissed out of hand."

"So you used me to nominate Caspar the Delinquent Ghost and Uncle Hugo nipped in with the challenge!"

"Once the trial by ordeal was in play the imprecise wording in the rule book could be exploited to allow females to compete."

I turned to my great-great-grandmama. "But why didn't you enter the contest yourself?"

"The ordeal might have been a feat of strength and at the age of one hundred and twenty I could hardly compete against a field of young persons. Your Aunt Hypatia, however, is at the peak of physical conditioning."

My aunt stroked Mrs. Beasely and preened a bit. "Carrying around the weight of these dresses with their attendant underpinnings would challenge Atlas himself if he were a woman."

I shook my head in wonder. "By Jakes, Bentley, I believe there is no nut you could not crack with that Olympian mind of yours. So, what happens now?"

My aunt stood. "Once I am sworn in as a member the precedent is set. The club charter will have to be altered to allow for female membership and your great-great-grandmother will be at the front of the line."

"Does this mean that any firstborn daughter of a member will be eligible?"

"We believe it does."

"That means Alice and Pansy will get in. Things are going to change quite a bit around the old place."

"And high time, too," harrumphed my aunt. "Men, like acid, are most destructive when they are concentrated. When sufficiently diluted by the civilizing presence of women, they are far less capable of doing harm."

I set down the can of cat food and Mrs. Beasely streaked over to delicately pick at it. "Poor Caspar will certainly never be a member now."

My aunt smiled. "That will be some salve for the wounds of the committee. Their relief at keeping him out may make them more welcoming of me."

I glanced at Bentley. "I suppose that was another facet of your stratagem?"

"It was, Sir."

A thought struck me. "But what if Caspar had accidentally found his way here before Aunt Hypatia?"

Bentley led me to a table in a corner of the room on which sat an extremely detailed model of the labyrinth. "That would have been impossible. The walls of the labyrinth are movable. Through a system of mirrors one can see anyone who enters and by the use of a few levers it is a simple matter to change the configuration of the maze in order to close off the cottage to any unwelcome visitor. That is how we guided you here, Sir."

I looked at him ruefully. "That explains the grinding noises. Herded me like a mouse, did you? Rather tarnishes the achievement, what?"

"I apologize, Sir, but you could never have found your way here by chance."

"Don't think of it, Bentley, it was all for the best."

My aunt gathered up Mrs. Beasely, who had licked the can of cat food clean. "I suppose we'd better go and inform the stewards that the challenge has been met. I await their groans with eager anticipation."

CHAPTER EIGHT

The Curse is Reversed

When Aunt Hypatia returned victorious, groans aplenty were certainly heaved but she was prepared to withstand them until the judgment day, so in the end the committee was forced to choke down its bile and admit that she had earned the right to membership. Cubby revealed the secret password to her through gritted teeth. He demonstrated the club handshake and taught her the secret whistle and door knock. We all joined in singing the club song a few times until she had the knack of it and the thing was done. She was a Twit!

Later that afternoon I lay sprawled in my armchair before the fire. The events of the day had utterly exhausted me. I was forced to admit that my aunt had right on her side. The benefit to my ancestor was a compelling argument in her favour and Bentley would hardly have assisted her if there was anything nefarious about the arrangement. One thing still nagged at me, however. There was an innocent party that I felt had been treated less than kindly and I was determined to put it right if I could.

Bentley slid into the room with a little cough. "Mr. Haspenhausen, Sir."

Caspar paced in close behind him. He threw himself into a chair and regarded me with a sardonic little smile. "Well, Chippy, it seems we were played like a couple of woodwinds by our dear aunt. I don't know about you but my hat's off to the old girl."

I rearranged the knickknacks on a nearby table nervously. "Yes, Aunt Hypatia usually succeeds in getting what she's after and woe betide those unfortunate enough to be in her way."

He gazed around the room appraisingly. "Nice digs you've got here. Look, if you called me here to apologize, don't bother. I couldn't care less about the test and all that. I'm quite happy as I am."

I faced him and straightened my spine. "But... oh, I say... are you? My aunt may regard you as something to be used and discarded but you are family. I have huddled with Bentley and I believe there may be a way to get you into the club after all."

He stared at me. "How on earth do you think you can accomplish that?"

"It's the recipe for the Naughty Vicar. It's one of the club's most tightly guarded secrets. Even Cubby doesn't know how it's done. I believe that if we threatened to release the recipe to the world the membership committee would rupture themselves hurrying to offer you membership."

Caspar sat back thoughtfully. I watched him as he stared into the fire. Finally, he shook his head. "It won't do, Chippy. The truth is, I never really wanted to be a member and if I blackmail my way in, they'll never let me forget it. I just don't belong there. Better let it go."

"And the recipe?"

"I'll keep it to myself if it would make things hot for you. I only ever make them for myself. Too expensive to hand them out to the freeloaders I run with."

I frowned unhappily. Perhaps there is something else... that is to say... can't I help you in some way?"

He stared at me with astonishment. "I believe you mean it! Chippy, you have unsuspected depths... but you're barking up the wrong tree."

"Am I?"

"You believe that the life you are living is the right and proper one and that I am a lost soul. I believe the positions are reversed. You go about like a wind-up toy, thoughtlessly engaging in ridiculous behavior to blind yourself to what is going on around you. I have no such illusions. When one sees the world for what it is, the only logical thing to do is to refuse to participate in the lies. That leaves very little for one to do except to drink and carouse and steal the hats off of policemen."

"What lies are you referring to?"

He leaned forward with an intensity I hadn't seen since we were nine and he had shaved my head while his friends held me down. "We've cocked it all up, Chippy. The world is burning. The people are starving. The animals are gone and we'll follow soon enough. All the cravats in the world won't change it."

"B-but we're going to fix it," I stuttered. "Smythe Corporation is working on it day and night. My Head of Social Justice, Judy, has got farms sprouting up everywhere. We're building desalination plants by the boatload... planting trees everywhere! We'll make the earth a paradise again!"

"Too late and even if you do, you and I won't be around to see it. It will take hundreds of years to undo the damage."

"Then we'll do it for our children's children. We've got to try to make things better, don't you see?"

He sat back and regarded me gravely. "You're a good egg, Chippy. All right, have your fun, but leave me alone with my bottle, won't you?"

I was flummoxed. I couldn't see any way to move him. The thought of Caspar returning to his life of debauchery was intolerable.

Bentley cleared his throat. "I believe it is time to feed the flock, Sir. Perhaps Mr. Haspenhausen would like to assist you."

Caspar looked at me curiously. "What's all that about? What flock are you feeding?"

I leaned in conspiratorially. "Look here, Caspar, you can't tell anyone about this. I've kept it a secret for reasons which will become clear to you. We had an adventure not long ago in the Northern Wilderness and... but come and see for yourself."

I led him to the back door. Bentley handed me a bucket of grain and we stepped into the back yard, where we found my small flock of clucking chickens wandering around the garden. Upon hearing the back door slam they made a mad dash for us and gathered around our ankles pecking and scratching eagerly. I scattered some grain and they happily tussled over it.

Caspar's eyes were like saucers. "I thought chickens were extinct!"

"Clearly not. We found a number of them being confined by cultists in the Northern Wilderness. After some harrowing adventures we were able to free them. I became quite attached to one particular little hen named Cackles. She bequeathed one of her eggs to me which I brought back at the end of our journey. When we arrived home, I discovered that Bentley had retrieved several more eggs from the wreckage of their poultry prison and we were able to hatch them. Their numbers are growing exponentially."

Caspar bent down and tentatively stroked a hen. She gently pecked his hand. Caspar laughed and sat right down in the middle of the flock. I scattered some grain on his tummy and in a moment, he was covered with clucking birds. I set the pail down by him and he happily fed them from his hand until the seeds were gone. Standing up with a sigh he brushed his hands and smiled.

"Cyril, I feel like a boy again."

Bentley stepped forward. "I wonder if Mr. Haspenhausen would be interested in the position of managing the new chicken preserve that Miss Judy is planning, Sir?"

Caspar turned to me eagerly. "A whole farm covered in chickens? It sounds like paradise!"

"Not a farm in the usual sense, of course. We don't intend to eat the chickens or their eggs. The point is to increase their numbers until the world can be repopulated with their offspring. Restore the balance of nature, what?"

"It's the nearest thing to Heaven I can imagine!"

"Well, look here Old Spout, the job is yours if you want it. It's fairly rugged out there for now—not much contact with civilization if you know what I mean."

"No newspapers, no magazines, no advertisements?"

"Just clean air and chickens as far as the eye can see."

"That's perfect. I'll take it!"

Later that evening, I gazed out my bedroom window at the gibbous moon while Bentley ran the warming pan around under the bedclothes.

"A good day's work, wouldn't you say, Bentley?"

"Quite satisfactory, Sir."

"Caspar is sorted out. That was a happy thought you had about the chickens."

"You would have thought of it in a moment, Sir."

"I imagine you're right."

"Your great-great-grandmother was quite impressed with you."

I smiled at the moon. "It is extremely gratifying to discover that one has a close relative whose existence was never guessed at."

"I believe you will find that Mrs. Chippington-Smythe is the best of relations. I hope it will make up in some small measure for the absence of your parents."

"Yes. One thought one was an orphan but that is no longer the case."

Bentley busied himself examining the warming pan before laying it by the fireplace. "Life is full of surprises, Sir. Who knows what tomorrow may bring?"

He pulled back the covers and I slipped under them. I snuggled into the warm sheets. "Good night, Bentley. It is good to have you home."

"It is good to be home, Sir."

He turned down the lamps and gently closed the door. I sighed and stared at the ceiling. Some part of me felt sad that my beloved club would never be quite the same. No more snapping towels at each other's genitals in the all-male steam room. No more drunken brawls with their resulting black eyes and split lips. The cabal of fez-wearing octogenarians that ran the committee would undoubtedly be infiltrated by the civilizing presence of female members. As I imagined Cubby Martinez trying to win an argument with my Aunt Hypatia, my mouth turned upward in a beatific smile and I drifted off into a deep, pleasant sleep.

THE END.

If you enjoyed this book, please
take a moment to visit

Amazon and provide a short
review; every reader's voice is
extremely important for the life
of a book or series.

If you'd like advance notice on the next book's
release head to:
WWW.TwitsChronicles.com
where you can sign up for my email list and where
you can ask Cyril and his friends a question which
they may choose to answer in a newsletter.
I hate spam as much as you do, so I will keep
emails to a minimum.

Keep an eye out for *Twits on the Stump,* coming
soon. Read on for a taste!

Loyal readers of these chronicles will have
gleaned that I, Cyril Chippington-Smythe,
believe "love" to be bunco. My nearest and
dearest have fallen prey to it over the years and
my response has been a haughty stare and a
supercilious sniff. My cousin Binky (Cheswick
Wickford-Davies to his creditors), however, falls

in love as though buying in bulk earns him a discount.

On this particular Spring day, he was composing odious odes and setting them to atonal melodies in honour of a young lady he had met at a pie shop. He was purchasing a porky pie and she was agitating for the rights of those who produced said pies.

Binky and I were lolling about in my richly appointed bedroom. I had gotten in the habit of staying in bed for most of the morning, sipping tea and munching on whatever Cook was inspired to bake. I was beginning to notice a small protuberance in my midsection, but the girdle took care of that. Bentley, my steam-powered valet, was gliding here and there keeping order and refilling teacups when necessary.

"What rhymes with Forsythia?"

I thought for a moment. "Galicia, if you pronounce it as they do in Santiago de Compostela."

He mumbled to himself for a moment and shook his head. "Too geographical."

"Arrythmia is rhyme adjacent."

He hummed something that sounded like a hive of mechanical bees in distress and sang in a kind of moan, "Show me some pity, my darling

Forsythia. You cause my heart to experience arrythmia."

"I beg you to stop."

"Wasn't there someone Greek named Pythia?"

Bentley cleared his throat. Bentley's mechanical brain is a miracle of technology and I have yet to see him stumped when information is required.

"That was the name given to one of the High Priestesses of ancient Greece, Sir. She was also known as the Oracle of Delphi."

Binky concentrated fiercely. "A song for the beautiful goddess Forsythia. You lay bare my future like the priestess called Pythia."

I groped about in the bedclothes until I found a slipper which I hurled at his head.

"One more rhyme and I shall have Bentley throw you down the stairs. No woman is worth it."

"You must meet her, Cyril. She is an angel."

"I've lost count of the number of angels you've introduced me to whose wings turned out to be made of sticks and muslin. Let me know when you meet an archangel and maybe I'll have a gander at her."

"You'll see, and then you'll eat your words."

I held out my cup for a top up.

"Bentley, your intelligence network is omnipresent. Do you know the young lady?"

Bentley straightened up with a small puff of steam. "May I ask her surname?"

"She was christened Forsythia Oblongata," Binky breathed reverently, "And she is a flower of womanhood."

"I have heard the name, Sir. She is descended from the Oblongatas of Kent. The family considers her to be something of a scandal. Her advocacy of political issues has caused them no little embarrassment."

Binky stared at Bentley icily. "She wishes to make the world a better place. She should be celebrated, not censured."

Bentley was unruffled. "I believe that her family's current objections arise from Miss Oblongata's attempt to unionize the hot pie industry. Oblongata's Prize Pies are the foundation of the Oblongata fortune, and the pie business has notoriously slim margins of profit. The salary and benefits that the workers are demanding would ruin them."

Binky raised a finger and recited, "Oblongata's Prize Pies is built upon a crust of lies!" He smiled modestly. "I came up with that one. Forsythia says that if they can't afford to pay their workers, then they must alter their way of doing business."

"The pie business is a cutthroat one, Sir. Their chief competitor, Bligh's Pies, would certainly take advantage."

I raised an eyebrow in Binky's direction. "She sounds like the usual fire and flood that attracts you, I must say."

His cheeks grew pink and his nostrils flared. "I will not hear a word against her. I know you think that my affections are too easily engaged but all that is in the past. I have found the one that fate intended for me and shall never love another."

I sat up against the pillows. "Some backbone at last! This Forsythia person may be doing you some good. Perhaps I should meet her after all."

"Of course, you should! I'm taking her to tea this afternoon. Why don't you join us?"

"Anything on the docket, Bentley?"

"You expressed a desire to have a depilatory applied to your back, Sir."

"That can wait. Tea, then."

"Goody!" Binky stood and brushed the crumbs from his lap. "We should toddle along. We're going to picket the pie shop for a bit and then hand out jars of fruity paste to the striking workers."

"Are they particularly fond of fruity paste?"

"I think it's more about the gesture... and the jars are nice."

I sighed and gave my scalp a vigorous rub. "Bentley, I shall rise and face the day."

Facing the day, as always, involved a grueling process of constricting my increasingly wobbly exterior with various straps and girdles to produce the tight tube of flesh that reflected the latest embodiment of male beauty. I gripped a heating pipe as Bentley hauled on the laces and whipped them into a complex knot to hold all steady.

I tested my ability to draw breath and was able to gasp, "That is sufficient. Thank you, Bentley."

Binky was bouncing on the balls of his trotters. "We mustn't be late. I don't want Forsythia to suspect a lack of zeal."

Bentley leaned in. "The Morning Cannon, Sir?"

I glanced at the clock. "Yes, it will only take a moment."

Binky groaned and threw himself into a chair.

Bentley wheeled the family cannon up to the firing window and threw up the sash. He wiped a smudge from the brass near the mouth of the old girl and inserted the charge, followed by the wadding. Wielding the rammer with practiced ease, he firmly settled all deep within the rifled tube and gave me a nod. I looked over at Binky.

"Care to do the honours?"

"I'll pass, thank you. Loud noises make me sneeze."

I grasped the lanyard. "What's the motto these days, Bentley?"

"Currently it is, 'Restore Our Former Glory,' Sir."

"Countdown please!"

Bentley looked inward at his mysterious timekeeping mechanism.

"Three, two, one, fire!"

I hollered, "Restore Our Former Glory," and yanked the cord. There was a satisfying "Boom!" which melded with my neighbours' artillery up and down the street. Screams of "Restore Our Former Glory" mingled in the Spring air, along with one confident shout of "Live Free or Die," which was followed a moment later by a sheepish "Restore Our Former Glory!"

I handed the lanyard to Bentley, who was already sponging out the heirloom, and turned to Binky.

"I am yours. *Avanti*!"

We exited the front door and I skidded to a halt at the sight of Binky's latest conveyance. It was a plain black sedan, but where the motor usually resided, there was a web of cords that stretched out in front of the vehicle. Each cord was fastened to a vest worn by one of a small platoon of athletic-looking young people who lounged about next to a flotilla of penny-farthing bicycles. Upon spotting Binky, they jumped to their feet and mounted their velocipedes.

"What is the meaning of this?"

He looked at me with delight. "It's my new automobile. Do you like it?"

"It's... it seems to be rather lacking something."

"What?"

"Well, an engine for a start. Could you not afford one? I would have lent you the money."

"Don't be ridiculous. This is the latest thing—human power."

"I thought progress had done away with that sort of thing. What of the steam engine? It is the culmination of man's ingenuity."

He made a dismissive noise. "Anyone can have a steam engine. Add water and hydrogen and away you go. When everyone has something, it is no longer worth having. I've created an entirely new arena and I have it all to myself for the moment. Isn't it chic?"

"I have nothing against it from an aesthetic point of view, but who are these persons attached to your automobile like a herd of those things that used to pull things? Peonies, was it?"

Bentley was easing the front door closed but he paused for a moment. "Ponies, Sir. A peony is a flower. A pony is a small horse."

I looked again at the bicyclists, who seemed to be rather champing at the bit. "What do you do with them when they're not pulling your car? What do you feed them? I say, aren't you rather oppressing them—forcing them to haul your carcass around like a pharaoh of old?"

"Not at all. They're a team, you see. They pedal for Eton. This is training for them. The whole thing is frightfully glamorous. Everyone at the club is scrambling to acquire a squad but I got the pick of the litter. Climb in."

We settled into our seats and Binky gave a wave to the lead bicyclist. "Oblongata's Pie Shop please, Dickie!"

The young man tipped his cap. "Right you are, Sir. Come on, team!" and off we sped. There were a few jerks as the cables grew taut and then we hummed along in an eerie silence with only the hiss of bicycle tires on pavement and the occasional barked order from Dickie to accompany us.

"Take up the slack there, Morrison! Miss Dlamini, are you training or perambulating to a picnic? Let's pick it up, Squad!"

The cyclists broke into what seemed to be their school pep song.

We pedal hard. We play it clean,
Our penny-farthings rule,
We ride our pitiless machines,
For country, Queen and school.

Eton College Cycling Team,
We'll ride until the end,
Our gears will grind, our brains will scheme,
We'll never, ever bend.

We alit before a structure which was adorned with a garish sign proclaiming "Oblongata's Prize Pies." Striking workers carrying placards trudged back and forth in front of the shop.

A mascot in a large pie costume capered next to the door. Upon spying me, the mascot carefully picked his way across the pavement and drew near.

"How nice to see you again, Sir," the pie said.

I peered into its eyeholes. "Compton?"

"Yes Sir, it's good old Compton. How nice of you to remember."

"When last we met, you were working as Cheeseworth's pet sheep."

"I've left the pet business, Sir. The meals were too irregular and included far too much grass, which plays havoc with the digestion."

"He mentioned a tour of some sort."

"Thoroughly Modern Millie, Sir. The production went bust in Cornwall. We're in the mascot business now."

"The whole family?"

"Oh yes. My wife is a chickeny nugget at Faux Poultry Palace and our Fred is a chip at a butty shop."

"Do give them my regards."

"I will, Sir. They'll be quite bowled over by your condescension. Are you purchasing a pie today? I can offer you a coupon for half off."

"I'm afraid not. I'm here in sympathy with the striking workers."

"I'm sorry to hear that. If they succeed in their demands, frills like mascots will be the first thing to go."

"Ah... well I have always admired your resourcefulness, Compton. I'm sure you'll land on your feet."

"That's what they said when I was hired to be a human cannonball, Sir, but it was seldom my feet that I landed on."

Binky was waving me over to a knot of protesters waving signs with sentiments such as "Workers arise, throw off your pies" and "We defy Prize Pies' lies."

As I approached, a placard that had been blocking my view slid aside and I beheld for the first time the countenance of Forsythia Oblongata. A sudden shock went through me, as though I had been shuffling over a luxurious woolen carpet while being rubbed vigorously with cats and had then reached for a lightning rod. My breath caught in my chest and my heart did a thumpa-thumpa sort of a thing. Was it love or angina? I felt no pain and smelled no burnt toast—thus I concluded that Cupid had landed a bullseye on the old ticker at last. I abandoned all propriety and gazed, slack-jawed, at the singular creature before me.

About The Author

Born in Canton, Ohio, and raised in a box made out of ticky-tacky, Tom Alan Robbins spent his youth as a middle-aged character actor. He has appeared in nine Broadway shows, including *The Lion King* in which he created the role of Pumbaa. He recently received a Grammy nomination for the cast album of *Little Shop of Horrors*. He has maintained a parallel career as a writer, penning scripts for TV shows like *Coach* and writing plays. His play, *Muse* won the New Works of Merit Playwriting Competition, and another play, *The Amish Girl's Guide to Armageddon*, won honorable mention in the 2020 Emerging Playwrights' Contest.

The Twits Chronicles series is his first attempt at novel writing and it has been a pure joy. He hopes to keep creating adventures for Cyril and Bentley as long as there are readers who enjoy them.

Also By Tom Alan Robbins

THE TWITS CHRONICLES:

Twits in Love

Twits in Peril

Twits Abroad

Twits on the Loose

Twits on the Hunt

Twits to the Test

Twits on the Stump

Twits Hit the Target

The Twits Chronicles: Anthology #1